Usborne Illustrated Traditional Stories

Usborne
Illustrated
Traditional
Stories

Illustrated by
Sara Gianassi

Contents

The Gingerbread Man

An old married couple lived together in the middle of the woods. They were mostly happy, but sometimes they felt sad that they didn't have a child.

One day the old woman decided to cheer herself up by doing some baking. She rolled out a piece of gingerbread and shaped it into a boy. She gave him chocolate chip eyes and a marshmallow nose, topping it all off with a wide smile made from strawberry icing.

After the old woman had finished, she gazed at her creation. "My sweet, little gingerbread man," she sighed. "If only you were real." This thought made her want a child more than ever, and she started to cry. A single teardrop fell onto the dough.

In a flash, the little gingerbread man stood up on his gingerbread legs. He hopped on one leg and then the other. The old woman staggered back, astonished.

"Our wishes have been answered," she gasped.

She looked around for her husband, but he was in the garden. As soon as her back turned, the little gingerbread man leaped off his plate and ran through the door.

"Stop little gingerbread man!" she called.

But he was too fast. As he ran into the garden, he sang in a sweet voice:

"Run, run, as fast as you can!
You can't catch me, I'm the gingerbread man!"

The old man outside couldn't believe his eyes. Was that a gingerbread man running across his lawn?

"Stop little gingerbread man! Stop, stop!" he called.

The gingerbread man was too fast for the old man. He was already among the trees when he turned to say, "I ran away from the woman and I can run away from you!"

The gingerbread man didn't stop there. He ran and ran until he came to a village school. The children saw him running across their playground. He looked delicious and their tummies rumbled hungrily.

"Stop little gingerbread man! Stop, stop!" they shouted. "We want to eat you!"

The children chased him across the playground and into the fields. They ran as fast as they could, but the gingerbread man was too fast. He was already in the fields when he sang in his sweet voice:

"Run, run as fast as you can!
You can't catch me, I'm the gingerbread man!"

With a cheeky grin, he added, "I've run away from the woman and the man and I can run away from you!"

The gingerbread man didn't stop there. He ran and ran until he came to a cow grazing in a meadow. "That gingerbread man looks much tastier than this grass," thought the cow, swallowing another green tuft.

"Stop little gingerbread man! Stop, stop!" she mooed. "I want to eat you!"

She chased him as fast as she could, but the gingerbread man was too fast. As he ran, he sang in a sweet voice:

"Run, run as fast as you can!
You can't catch me, I'm the gingerbread man!"

With a cheeky grin, he added, "I've run away from the woman, the man and the children and I can run away from you!"

The gingerbread man didn't stop there. He ran and ran until he came to a horse in a stable. This horse had never seen anything that looked so delicious.

"Stop little gingerbread man! Stop, stop!" neighed the horse. "I want to eat you!"

The horse galloped as fast as he could, but the gingerbread man was too fast.

He was nearly at the river when he sang in his sweet voice:

"Run, run as fast as you can!
You can't catch me, I'm the gingerbread man!"

Then the gingerbread man's cheeky grin vanished. He could see the river was too wide to jump across. It wouldn't be long before the horse, the cow, the children, the man and the woman caught up with him.

"What can I do?" cried the gingerbread man. "There's nowhere to go."

"I might be able to help you," said a bright-eyed fox with a silky voice. "I can take you across this river."

"I'm sure you can," said the gingerbread man. "But don't you want to eat me?"

"Why would I want to eat you?" asked the fox. "You don't look that tasty to me."

"Well, if you promise," said the gingerbread man. "But I'll ride on your tail just to be safe."

"Be my guest," replied the fox.

They were halfway across the river, when the fox's tail started to sink.

"Oh no!" cried the gingerbread man. "I'm getting soggy."

"I'm sorry my friend, this river is deep," the fox replied. "Why don't you jump on my back? It'll be dry there."

The gingerbread man jumped on the fox's back. He didn't have much choice as the water was rising quickly.

The gingerbread man jumped on the fox's back.

As the fox waded deeper, even his back became wet.

"I'm sorry my friend, I'll have to swim from here. Why don't you jump on my nose? It'll be dry there."

The gingerbread man jumped on the fox's nose. He really didn't want to get wet, so what choice did he have?

Before long, they had reached the other side. The gingerbread man was so relieved, he jumped for joy.

This was the moment the fox had been waiting for. As he climbed out of the water, he tossed the gingerbread man in the air with his nose. The little gingerbread man fell straight into the fox's wide open mouth. It was full of sharp teeth.

Snap!

The gingerbread man was a quarter gone!

Snap! Snap!

The gingerbread man was half gone!

Snap! Snap! Gulp!

"Well," said the fox, "he was even tastier than he looked." With that, he licked the last few gingerbread crumbs off his lips and padded off into the afternoon sun.

The Three Billy Goats Gruff

Once upon a time there were three billy goat brothers named Gruff. They lived happily in a meadow on the mountainside until, at last, they found the grass was getting short and bare. All that was left to eat was a few thistles.

"My stomach is rumbling," grumbled the biggest billy goat.

"I can't even remember what clover tastes like," complained the middle billy goat.

"We need to find more food," decided the littlest billy goat. He trotted into the forest, and his brothers followed one by one.

After a short journey, the littlest billy goat came to an old stone bridge that arched over a fast-flowing river. Stretching away on the far side of the bridge was a meadow. But it was no ordinary meadow. The deep grass was dotted with wildflowers. Streams tumbled through beds of leafy clover, and the little goat could hear bees buzzing inside the buttercups.

"This way, brothers," he cried, and he hurried onto the bridge.

Clippity-clop, clippity-clop, went the goat's hooves on the stones. But the cheerful sound fell on wicked ears. In the shadows under the bridge, there lived an old troll. He had been sleeping among some boulders, and now he woke with a start.

"Who's that clippity-clopping over my bridge?" he growled. With one kick of his hairy feet, he jumped up onto the bridge, and blocked the way across.

"Snick, snack, crick, crack!" he sang, reaching for the goat. "Why, you're hardly big enough to call breakfast."

"Oh, Mr. Troll," said the little billy goat, dancing away from the troll's claws, "you're right. I'm far too small to eat. A single mouthful such as me would only make your hunger sharper, and my tiny bones would stick in your teeth."

The troll frowned as the nimble billy goat again leaped out of his grasp.

"One mouthful is better than none," he insisted.

"Yes," replied the goat, "but two are better than one. Soon my older brother, who is twice as big as me and *much* juicier, will come across this bridge. Hadn't you better wait and eat him instead?"

This made good sense to the greedy troll. He licked his lips with a long, green tongue and let the little goat pass. The goat cantered happily into the meadow, while the troll ducked beneath his bridge to wait.

Soon, the middle billy goat Gruff trotted out of the forest. **Clip-clop, clip-clop, clip-clop,** went his hooves on the stones of the bridge – and again, the troll jumped out of the shadows and blocked the way.

"Mish, mash, bish, bash!" he sang, clacking his claws together. "Your brother was right. You look like a plump little breakfast for a hungry troll."

"Oh, Mr. Troll," said the middle billy goat, dodging out of the troll's reach, "I may be a good-sized goat, but I fear I would only spoil your appetite. Soon my older brother will come across this bridge. He's twice as big as me and *much* tastier. Hadn't you better wait and eat him instead?"

The thought of an even bigger breakfast was too hard to resist, and the troll had to wipe a bit of slobber from his warty chin.

"Very well," he said, and again he let the billy goat pass.

He ducked back under the bridge, dreaming of the fattest, tastiest goat of all. Would he bake it in a pie? Or gulp it down, hair and all?

Soon enough, the biggest billy goat Gruff trotted out of the forest. **Clomp, clomp, clomp,** went his hooves on the stones, and the sound echoed down into the riverbed. For the third time, the troll jumped up onto the bridge and blocked the way.

"Shiver, shake, quiver, quake!" he sang, rolling his beady eyes. "Here you are at last – the best and biggest billy goat of all. I'm going to eat you right up."

"You'll do no such thing, you rude troll," replied the billy goat.

"Yes, I will," insisted the troll. But now that they were face to face, he noticed that this billy goat looked much stronger than his brothers. He also looked much fiercer, with his curving horns and sharp, sturdy hooves. Suddenly, the troll wasn't feeling quite so confident. Perhaps the littlest billy goat would have made a better meal after all? But now it was too late.

Before the troll could turn and run, the goat gave a mighty stamp, lowered his horns and thwacked him right in the chin. The wicked troll tumbled back and tripped over the side of his bridge. Then, with a mighty splash, he plunged into the deepest, swiftest part of the river. The water swirled around him, whisking him downstream.

With a mighty splash, he plunged into the deepest, swiftest part of the river.

"Glub, blub, blub," the troll cried. All trolls hate to bathe, and he could feel the river weeds scrubbing his skin, and the current clearing out the muck from between his toes. He bumped through rapids and tumbled over waterfalls. Hours later, when he dragged himself ashore, he was as clean and fresh as a baby.

The troll found a new bridge to make his home. But from that day forward, whenever he heard the **clippity-clop, clippity-clop** of little hooves on the stones above, he hid his head among the boulders and waited quietly until they'd passed.

The three billy goats Gruff were reunited and lived happily ever after in their new meadow. There, they ate their fill of grass and clover until even the littlest one was big, strong, and more than a match for trolls.

The
Three
Aunts

Long ago, in a little cottage deep in the woods, there lived a poor man. His wife had died young, so he lived quite alone except for his daughter, and made his living as best he could from hunting in the woods.

"Father," said his daughter one day, as she stirred the stew for supper, "you know I love you, but I've lived all my life in these woods and have never seen anything beyond them. I am old enough now to look after myself. Please, let me go and see the world."

"I knew this day would come," her father sighed, as he made up the fire under the cooking pot. "It hasn't been much of a life for you. You can cook, but I couldn't teach any of the other skills young ladies should have. Who knows how you'll earn a living? Yet I can't keep you when you long to go. See the world, with my blessing."

And so the girl set off. She walked through the woods, following the rough track until the trees grew thin and small and gave way to sunlit meadows, filled with buttercups. The path became broader now, and ran between fields golden with whispering wheat, almost ready for harvest. Soon, it led to a village, with trim little houses lining the road. The girl smiled to herself, delighted with everything she saw.

At the edge of the village, she stopped short. There, surrounded by high railings and beautiful gardens, was a palace with smooth, white walls and polished windows that glinted in the sunshine.

As the girl stood there gazing, a man came to the gate. "You'll be here for the kitchen maid job?" he said, and opened the gate without waiting for a reply.

Before the girl knew what was happening, she was following him around to the side of the palace and into the kitchen.

A brisk, red-cheeked cook put the girl to work right away. "We're short-handed today," she explained, "so you must do the best you can." The girl worked hard, chopping and pounding, stewing and frying, just as her father had taught her. Then, she washed the dishes.

"I wish we had more workers like you," the cook said, wiping her hands on her apron at the end of the day. "You get more done in a day than some do in weeks."

The other maids stood in a cluster, eyeing the girl angrily and whispering. "I suppose she thinks she can do anything now," said the dairy maid. "I'd like to see her try!" added the laundry maid. "We'll show her," they agreed, and crept off to spread the word.

By the following morning, the girl was the talk of the palace.

"I've heard she can scrub out a greasy cauldron in five minutes," whispered the footman to the butler.

"I've heard she can sew a shirt in an hour," muttered the butler to the lady-in-waiting.

"I've heard she can spin a pound of flax into fine linen thread in a day," murmured the lady-in-waiting to the Queen.

The Queen clapped her hands with delight. She loved spinning, weaving and sewing. "Bring the girl here, I must meet her!" she cried.

The girl was shown into the Queen's grand drawing room. She stood there trembling, wondering what terrible thing she had done to be sent for by the Queen herself. But the Queen smiled and patted her hand.

"Everyone says you can spin a pound of flax into fine linen thread in a day, my dear," she cooed. "You must show me – I can't wait to see how you do it so fast."

"Um, Your Majesty," mumbled the girl, turning very pink, "I can't... I'm not sure..."

"There, there," said the Queen kindly. "You're shy, I can see. You'll have a room all to yourself – no one will be watching. I'll arrange it all."

"But, Your Majesty," the girl tried again, turning red, "I mean... I don't know..."

"You're too modest!" The Queen laughed. "Now, it's all settled. You'll have till this time tomorrow – we won't rush you. But if you can't manage it by then, well, there's no room in this palace for liars. Show her to her room!"

The girl followed a lady-in-waiting to a room. It was empty except for a chair, a bed and a spinning wheel with a pound of flax piled next to it on the floor. As the door closed behind her, the girl burst into tears. She had no idea what to do. She had never even *seen* a spinning wheel before, let alone used one.

"Why are you crying, my dear?" came a scratchy voice. The girl looked around and saw a very strange old woman opening the door. Her nose was longer and more bent than any the girl had ever seen, but her eyes twinkled kindly.

"I'm in such trouble," sobbed the girl, and poured out the whole story.

The old woman smiled brightly. "It's your lucky day!" she said. "I can help you. In fact, I'll spin the flax for you."

The girl stopped crying in astonishment. "Thank you!" she replied. "But how can I ever make it up to you?"

"Well," said the old woman, sitting down at the spinning wheel and setting to work, "I will ask just one thing. On the happiest day of your life, call me 'Aunt'."

This seemed an odd request, but the girl was so grateful to the strange old woman, and she couldn't see how it could do any harm.

"It's the least I can do," she replied.

"Good girl!" cried the old woman. "Now, you can just have a nap. There's nothing more for you to do."

When the girl woke, it was morning. The old woman had gone, but there, on the chair, was a big skein of fine linen thread. Just then, the Queen looked in.

"You've finished!" she said, admiring the thread. "You really are as good as they say," she added. "Speaking of which, I've heard that you can weave all this thread into smooth linen cloth in just a day. So quick and clever! Do show me, there's a dear."

Once again, the girl tried to explain that she couldn't, but it was no good. The Queen was quite determined.

"Here you are," said the Queen triumphantly, as two servants carried a massive loom into the room. "You'd better start right away."

Once again, as the door shut, the girl felt

Two servants carried a massive loom into the room.

tears trickling down her face. But, right then, she heard a strange, squeaky voice, saying, "What is the matter, my dear?"

Another old woman was looking in at the door. Her shoulders were hunched up around her ears and her back was bent, but she was smiling merrily. The girl told all her troubles.

"Don't worry," said the old woman kindly. "I'll do it for you." And she sat down at the loom and started to weave.

"How can I ever repay you?" asked the girl.

"There is something," the old woman replied. "On the happiest day of your life, call me 'Aunt'."

The girl was surprised to receive this request again, but she agreed, and was soon fast asleep while the old woman wove away.

The girl awoke to find a smooth length of cloth neatly folded on the chair. Once again, the Queen was delighted. "Well, I almost believe those people who've told me you can sew all that cloth into shirts in just one day. But you must show me."

The girl found herself alone in the room once more, with needles, pins and scissors. And, again, she started to cry. At once, a croaky voice said, "What seems to be the matter, my dear?"

This time, the girl was no longer surprised to see an unusual old woman standing in the doorway. This one had huge, bulging eyes, but she was nodding sympathetically. So, of course, the girl told her the problem.

"Don't fret! I can sew the shirts for you,"

the old woman reassured her. "But, please, on the happiest day of your life, call me 'Aunt'."

The girl agreed right away, and drifted off to sleep while the old woman snipped, pinned and stitched the cloth.

The next morning, the girl found a pile of elegant shirts on the chair. She wondered what further task the Queen might set her now, but she needn't have worried.

"You've well and truly proved your skill," the Queen cooed happily as she examined the shirts. "I'd be proud to have you as my daughter. You'd be able to keep the whole family in thread, cloth and clothing, with no help at all."

There was a gentle cough and a handsome young man edged around the Queen.

"Do you mean that, Mother?" he asked. "Because if so, I have an important question to ask..." The Prince sank to one knee in front of the girl. "Will you marry me?" he said.

In just a few weeks, the wedding day arrived. The girl was dizzy with happiness for the Prince proved to be as kind as he was handsome. Her only worry was how she would manage to do all the spinning, weaving and sewing the Queen had in mind for her – but she tried to forget about that. After all, it was supposed to be the happiest day of her life.

Just as all the guests were sitting down to the wedding feast, the girl heard a familiar, scratchy voice. There was the first old woman, her long nose looming across the table. "Well, my dear?" she said.

The girl remembered her promise. "Welcome, Aunt," she said, promptly. The Prince looked surprised, but he quickly made room for the old woman at the table.

"Any Aunt of my beloved bride's is welcome at her wedding," he said.

Just as everyone was starting to eat, the girl heard two more voices – one squeaky and one croaky. "Well, my dear?" said the second old woman, her hunched back casting a vast shadow on the wall. The third old woman's bulging eyes glittered in the candlelight.

"Welcome, Aunts," said the girl. Once again, the Prince made a space for them to sit down. He chatted politely to the three Aunts, but all the while his eyes kept flicking from them to his bride. At last, he couldn't hold his thoughts in any longer.

"My dear ladies," he began, "you are all most welcome. But I must admit that if I had not heard my bride call you her aunts, I wouldn't have recognized you. You don't exactly..." he coughed politely, "um... look like her."

"Well," said the first old woman, "I looked just like your beautiful bride when I was her age, but since then I've spent so many hours nodding over my spinning wheel that my nose has just grown and grown."

"Yes," chipped in the second old woman, "in my case it was hunching over my loom all day that turned my back from straight to bent."

"And with me," added the third, "it was straining my poor eyes over fine needlework that made them bulge so."

"Well," the Prince declared, "I'll make sure my dearest bride will never suffer in that way. From now on, she never need touch a spinning wheel, loom or needle again."

The girl sighed blissfully. Now it truly was the happiest day of her life.

The Little Red Hen

One day a little red hen was scratching around in the farmyard when she came across a large pile of seed.

"Hmm. Looks like wheat," she clucked to herself. "It would be a pity to let it go to waste. I think I'll plant it."

There was rather a lot of it for one little red hen to plant all on her own. She looked around the farmyard. There, sitting in the shade of a tree, was a dog.

"Dear dog, will you help me plant these seeds?" she asked.

"Not I," said the dog. "It's far too hot for me to be running around planting seed. Ask the cat."

The cat was lying stretched out in the full sun, and couldn't have been happier if she'd had a big bowl of cream.

"Cat, will you help me plant the seeds?" asked the little red hen hopefully.

"Not I. The soil will dirty my white paws," the cat replied. "And I've only just washed them," she added, licking her paw lazily.

The only other animal in the farmyard was the duck, who was splashing noisily in a tub of water.

"I don't suppose you'll help me, will you?" the red hen asked.

"Quack, quack, quack. I'd love to help you..."

"Oh *thank you* duck!" the hen began, her face lighting up.

"But," the duck interrupted, "I am having a bath right now. Sorry!"

So, the little red hen shrugged and went off to plant her seeds on her own. It took her the rest of the afternoon. By the time she had finished she was exhausted.

Weeks went by, and the seeds sprouted and grew into tall, strong spears of golden wheat. The little red hen looked with satisfaction at her crop, as it waved in the gentle breeze. 'But I'll never harvest it all on my own,' she thought.

Just then, the dog trotted past, looking as though he were on an important mission. But the little red hen knew better.

"Hello dog! See how well my wheat has grown. It's already ready to harvest. Will you help me?"

"Ha! Not I," barked the dog. "Can't you see I am busy?"

"Busy doing *what*?" asked the hen.

"Oh, you know," the dog answered vaguely.

"Things to do, people to see..." He didn't even pause to stop and talk.

The cat was sitting nearby, washing her tail.

"Cat, I don't suppose…"

"Meow," replied the cat. "Sorry. I'm busy too, and besides, I might blunt my claws on the wheat."

The little red hen didn't have much hope that the duck would help, but she asked all the same.

"Sorry," the duck quacked without looking the least bit sorry at all. "I'm giving my ducklings swimming lessons in a few minutes."

The little red hen said nothing. She knew full well that the duck's ducklings had long since grown and were perfectly capable of swimming without help, and certainly didn't need lessons.

So the little red hen harvested the wheat all by herself.

So the little red hen harvested the wheat all by herself. It took almost until nightfall.

The next day, she knew there wasn't much point in asking if the dog, the cat or the duck would help her to carry the heavy bag of wheat to the mill to get it ground into flour. But she did so all the same.

"Not I," said the dog. "Far too busy."

"Not I," said the cat. "Too sleepy."

"Not I," said the duck. "Too wet, and the flour will just stick to my feathers."

So the little red hen took the wheat to the mill by herself, and when it had been ground into flour, she dragged the heavy sack all the way back to the farm, all on her own.

Later on, she looked around the farmyard once again.

"Right. Now who's going to help me bake this flour into some tasty bread?" she asked.

"Not I," barked the dog.

"Not I," meowed the cat.

"Not I," quacked the duck.

The little red hen just shrugged. She dragged the flour into the kitchen and made some bread.

When the bread came out of the oven, a mouthwatering aroma wafted into the farmyard. In the blink of an eye, the dog and the cat and the duck appeared around the kitchen table.

"Now," clucked the hen. "*Who* is going to help me eat this delicious freshly baked loaf of bread?"

"Me!" woofed the dog.

"Me too," meowed the cat.

"Me, me, me," quacked the duck.

"Oh no you are not," said the hen. "None of you were prepared to help me when there was work to be done, so now I am going to eat it all myself!"

And that's exactly what she did.

The Mouse's Wedding

Not so long ago in Japan there lived a family of three mice. Mother and Father Mouse always said to anyone who would listen that they were the happiest mice in the world. Their daughter was clever, kind and beautiful, and their only worry was that they would never find any mouse good enough to marry her.

"We must only part with our darling if we can find someone who truly deserves her," said Mother Mouse to Father Mouse one bright spring morning.

They watched their daughter chatting and giggling with the handsome young mouse who lived in the house along the way. "Of course, Daichi from next door is the very best of mice. But for our dearest child, I'm beginning to think that no mere mouse will do."

Father Mouse agreed. "Our daughter is as graceful and beautiful as this cherry blossom," he said, looking up to the tree flowering over their heads. "I think only the very greatest and most glorious of husbands could make her truly happy."

The longer Mother and Father Mouse

talked it over, the surer they became. They would seek out the most brilliant, powerful and eligible suitor in the world, and introduce him to their daughter. The only problem was how to find him.

Mother and Father Mouse talked some more. And then some more. They discussed it as they watched the little mice with their fish-shaped streamers in May. They debated it as they danced in the warm summer night under glowing paper lanterns in July. They considered it as they admired the rich tones of chrysanthemum flowers in September. And they wondered about it as they listened to the temple bells ringing out the end of December and the start of the New Year.

They were walking home through the crisp,

dark New Year night when Father Mouse suddenly stopped and looked up at the sky.

"Of course!" he cried. "Why did it take me so long to realize? It's obvious when you think about it. The brightest, best and most powerful of all is the Sun. He can turn gloomy night into dazzling day and banish the cold in an instant. We must go to meet him and introduce him to our daughter!"

The next fine day, Mother and Father Mouse set off to talk to the Sun. Wearing their warmest clothes, they walked through gently sloping fields and past thatched farmhouses, until they came to the foot of the mountain. Then, they started the climb.

After several hours of weary trudging, the trees started to thin out and the air became thick and white as the mice passed through a layer of cloud hugging the mountain's sides.

As they climbed higher, the trees grew even fewer and further between, until there were none at all. Then the air cleared and the mice stepped into the bright sunshine. They had reached the top at last, and it was just midday, so the Sun was right above them. Standing on tiptoe on the highest peak, they squeaked as loudly as they could to attract his attention.

"Oh Sun! Would you care to meet our delightful daughter?" they asked. "She's just the right age to be married, and she surpasses all other mice in beauty, wisdom and kindness. So we thought that you, the most brilliant and powerful in all the world, would be just the right type of husband to make her happy."

The Sun heard a faint squeaking noise and looked down from the sky. Hearing what the mice had in mind, he hid a smile. How could he ever marry a tiny mouse? But he was determined not to hurt their feelings and shone down on the little mice kindly.

"It is very good of you to make me this offer," he replied, "but I must confess that I am not as powerful as you suggest. After all, as soon as a cloud passes in front of me, he blocks my warmth and light."

"That's very true," the mice agreed. "We hadn't thought of that. So the Cloud must be the best and most important, then. We will go to speak with him."

With that the two little mice set off down the mountainside. Soon, they passed into the layer of thick, white cloud. They waved their arms around so the Cloud would notice them, and then squeaked very clearly.

"Oh Cloud! Please do consent to meet our

dearest daughter," they cried. "We're sure you'd like her. Her intelligence, charm and beauty are unsurpassed. So we thought that you, the mightiest in all the world, would make the best husband for her."

The Cloud heard the two little mice squeaking in his midst. 'What fond parents,' he thought to himself. 'Their idea would never work, but, after all, they only want the best for their daughter.' So he thought of a reply that would not disappoint them too much.

"Good mice," he boomed, "I am flattered that you're making me this proposal. But I must admit that there is someone much more powerful than myself. The wind only has to blow a little, and I must go scudding across the sky in whatever direction he chooses."

"Well," the mice replied, "that does make sense now you come to mention it. The Wind must be the strongest after all! We will go and find him and see what he says."

Although they were up so high, there was no wind, so they headed down the mountainside. Going downhill was much quicker, so they soon reached the gently sloping fields once more. But there was no wind there, either.

"I know," said Mother Mouse. "Let's go to the seashore. I believe the Wind can often be found there."

So they set off, across fields, through woods and over streams, until they reached the coast. They stood there, looking out over the dancing waves and feeling a fresh breeze on their faces. Then, bowing politely, they spoke.

"Oh Wind! Can we invite you to visit our beloved daughter? She is not only gifted but attractive and respectful too. You are the greatest and strongest in the world, so we hoped that you would be a fitting husband for her."

The Wind chuckled to himself as he played with the frilly little waves along the shoreline.

'Where on Earth did those little mice get that idea?' he asked himself, but when he answered, he whispered soothingly in the mice's ears.

"I am sure your daughter is the best and most accomplished of maidens, and deserves the finest husband," he assured them, "but you do me too much kindness. I am not the strongest. Just think how little power I have

"Oh Wind! Can we invite you to visit our beloved daughter?"

compared to the wall of a house, such as the one you live in. I can blow and blow, but still the wall doesn't fall down."

The mice bowed once again to the Wind.

"You're right, we see that now," they told him. "We must go home to our house and consult our very own Wall, and see if he would like to marry our daughter."

So they walked home as fast as they could, and arrived at their house just as dusk was falling. Losing no time, they stood in front of the Wall and tapped it gently with their paws.

"Oh Wall," they squeaked, "you are surely the strongest and most upstanding in the whole world. We have been searching for the best and most powerful husband for our darling daughter. She is as beautiful as she is kind and clever, you can't fail to be pleased with her. Can we interest you in her hand in marriage?"

The Wall wondered how best to reply to this strange request. He knew the mice well, and didn't want to make fun of them.

"My dear little friends," he began, "I have seen your daughter grow up, and I know her charm, wit and good nature well. I only regret that I am not all you think me. How can I be the strongest when little mice can nibble holes in me?"

Mother and Father, once again, could see that they had been wrong.

"So it's mice who are the strongest of all!" they cried. And they scampered off to give their daughter the good news.

As they came around the corner of the wall, they caught sight of her laughing and chatting with Daichi, the handsome young mouse from next door. Mother Mouse turned to Father Mouse thoughtfully.

"You know, we have always said that Daichi is the very best of mice. Perhaps he and our daughter could be happy together?"

Father Mouse agreed – and, more importantly, so did the two young mice.

So they were married that spring, just as the cherry trees blossomed. And no mice have ever been happier together, from that day to this.

Baba Yaga

Anna lived with her father and stepmother in a pretty little cottage in the middle of the woods.

She was a very kind little girl. She was kind to everyone and everything. She was kind to her father and her school friends. She was kind to her toys. She was even kind to the little field mouse who lived under her doorstep. Every day she would leave the mouse some milk and a few cake crumbs from her afternoon tea.

She was so kind, it was a shock to find that some people, like her stepmother, could be unkind.

Anna's stepmother was beautiful, but she was also cruel. She would make impossible demands and then punish Anna when she didn't meet them.

One day, when Anna's father was out hunting, her stepmother asked her to pick up a needle and thread from Baba Yaga in the woods.

When Anna heard Baba Yaga's name, she shuddered, knocking over her glass of milk.

"B...B...Baba Yaga? Isn't she the witch with iron teeth?" she stuttered.

"How dare you talk back to me?" shouted her stepmother. "Clean up this mess right now, and then be off with you!"

Anna got down to clean up. Under the table, she saw her friendly field mouse had come to lap up the milk. She started to cry.

"I'm sorry to cry, little mouse," she sobbed. "I'm just very frightened of Baba Yaga. I've heard that she eats children."

"Don't worry, dear girl," squeaked the mouse. "I can tell you a secret that will keep you safe. You have a kind heart. Take that with you, and be sure to pick up everything that you find on your journey. If you do that, I promise you'll come to no harm."

Anna was very grateful. After she had let the mouse drink all the milk, she set off.

Not long into her journey, Anna came across a pink ribbon lying on the ground.

Remembering the mouse's words, she bent down and picked it up.

Further along, she picked up a small blue oil can. Then, as the woods grew thicker, she found some scraps of ham. She added them to her bundle.

As she crept deeper into the forest, it grew dark, and the wind started to howl. Anna knew this meant that Baba Yaga was nearby. She backed against a tree and waited.

Soon, she caught sight of a long black shadow. Anna gasped. It was Baba Yaga, flying through the trees in a heavy black cauldron. Her arms were thin and bony, but her eyes were bright like red hot coals.

She must have been very strong. In one hand she held a wooden spoon that was longer

Baba Yaga

It was Baba Yaga, flying through the trees in a heavy black cauldron.

than Anna was tall. In the other, she swished a heavy broom to wipe away her tracks.

Anna watched as the witch disappeared behind a high gate. To go through it herself, Anna had to squeeze past the prickly branches of a sad looking holly tree. Even though it scratched her badly, Anna felt sorry for anything that lived so close to Baba Yaga. She decorated the tree with her pink ribbon.

"Perhaps this will cheer you up," she said as she tied a bow around one of its branches. "How lucky I picked up this ribbon."

Anna moved on, pushing her way through the gate. As it opened, the rusty hinges made a terrible screeching sound.

"Oh dear, you poor old gate," Anna sighed. "How lucky I picked this up too," she added as she took out her blue can to pour oil over the squeaky hinges.

As soon as she entered the yard, Anna noticed Baba Yaga's small, wooden hut. But this was no normal hut. It didn't stand still like huts were supposed to. It was moving around the yard, hopping from one foot to the other. Anna rubbed her eyes in disbelief. As she looked closer, she saw the hut stood on long, spindly chicken legs.

In a flash, the chicken-legged hut spun around so it was facing her. An ear-splitting cry rang through the air, calling Baba Yaga's name like a rooster. Anna looked around before realizing that the hut itself was making the sound.

Baba Yaga came to the window, gnashing

her iron teeth. "Fie, fie, what brings the smell of children to my yard?" she cackled.

"If you please," Anna replied, "my stepmother sent me to ask you for a needle and thread."

"Very well," crowed the witch. "But you'll have to do a few things for me in return. If you succeed, I'll see what I can do. If you fail, I'll eat you for lunch. First, take this jug and fill my bathtub with water from the stream. It's about time for my yearly wash."

Anna gulped when she saw there was a hole in the jug. No matter how quickly she ran, all the water would leak out before she reached the bathtub.

On her way to the stream, Anna spotted a very thin cat prowling around the yard.

"Poor thing, you look hungry," she said as she stopped to feed him the ham from her bundle. "How lucky I picked this up."

"Can I make a suggestion?" purred the cat, after he'd finished eating.

"Oh yes please," said Anna. "I don't know how I shall fill the bathtub with this jug."

"Why don't you block the hole with some clay from the ground?" he mewed.

"What a clever cat!" Anna said, stroking his head before setting to work.

When Baba Yaga saw the full bathtub, she raised a wispy eyebrow.

"I'm impressed little girl," she said. "But I see you used the clay from my yard. That reminds me: last week I spilled a bag of sugar out there. I'd like you to pick up every single grain while I relax in this bath."

Anna knew it was a hopeless task, just like the ones her stepmother would set. Baba Yaga was surely going to eat her.

Just then, she felt the cat nudging her leg. "Psst," the cat whispered. "You'll never pick up every grain... But I can help you escape."

"Oh yes please, dear cat," said Anna. "But how? Baba Yaga is much too fast for me."

"Purrrrhaps," said the cat. "But I have a few tricks up my sleeve."

He produced a mirror and a comb. "Baba Yaga will chase you. When the wind grows stronger, it means she's close. Throw down this mirror to slow her down. If she comes again, throw down this comb."

Anna didn't understand how a mirror or a comb could help her, but she trusted the cat. It was time to make her escape.

When she opened the gate, the oiled hinges didn't make a sound. Outside, the holly tree gracefully parted its branches, just for her. She slipped away silently, and without a scratch.

Baba Yaga looked around for Anna when she finished her bath.

"Where's my little girl?" she shrieked at the cat. "Where's my lunch?"

"She has run away madam. I helped her. She was kind to me and gave me ham. You've never given me food."

Baba Yaga screamed and ran outside. She looked at the gate and growled, "Why didn't you squeak, you rust bucket?"

"She was kind to me, madam," it replied. "She oiled my hinges. You've never done that."

"Why didn't you block her path, you worthless twig?" she howled at the holly tree.

"Because she was kind to me too," it said. "She tied this pretty pink ribbon to my branch. You've never done that."

Baba Yaga roared so loudly that the woods themselves shook.

As she was running away, Anna felt the wind grow stronger. Baba Yaga was close. She remembered the cat's words and threw the mirror behind her. It shattered into shards that became water droplets that grew into a wide, flowing river. It blocked the witch's path entirely.

"Rats!" cursed Baba Yaga. "But she won't stop me so easily. If I drink it dry, I can still catch the girl."

With that, she bent down and started to drink gallons of water at a time in huge, long slurps. She drained the entire river in minutes.

Before long Anna felt the wind grow stronger again. When she heard the thud of the spoon and the swish of the broom, she threw down her comb.

Immediately the comb grew into a thick forest. Baba Yaga's cauldron got caught in the undergrowth. Vines twisted around her spoon. Brambles tangled in her broom. She was stuck. The witch shrieked with rage.

Anna didn't look back. She ran all the way home, straight into her father's arms.

"What on Earth's the matter, my dear little girl?" he asked with a worried frown.

"Baba Yaga tried to eat me," Anna panted. "Stepmother sent me to her hut for a needle and thread!"

Before Anna's father had a chance to speak, they heard the front door slam shut. Anna and her father watched as her stepmother ran away, jumping over the garden fence. The last they ever saw of her was a long dark shadow disappearing into the woods.

From that day, nothing disturbed Anna's peaceful life. Nothing, that is, except the odd visit from her friendly field mouse, who was always greeted with plenty of cake and milk whenever he came to the door.

The Boy who Cried Wolf

There once was a shepherd boy named Rufus. He was supposed to look after a little flock of sheep, but he wasn't very good at it. He never paid attention when the sheep wandered off, got tangled up in brambles, or fell into a brook and got their fleeces muddy.

Rufus didn't care much about sheep. He would much rather have spent his days pulling faces and playing pranks with the other boys from the village.

One morning, Rufus took his flock to a meadow above the village, right at the edge of the forest. He sat in the tall grass surrounded by munching sheep and felt himself getting more... and more... and more bored.

"Argh!" Rufus moaned. "It's so quiet! If only something would happen."

The sheep ignored him. Down in the valley, everything was calm. The farmer was tending her rows of cabbages and lettuces, and the baker was kneading dough by an open window. The distant **ping, ping, ping,** of the blacksmith's hammer meant that he was hard at work in his forge.

"I'll bet they could use some excitement," Rufus said to himself. Grinning, he thought of a prank to play on them. He jumped up on a rock and cupped his hands around his mouth.

"Wolf!" he called – and, louder, "WOLF! Help! There's a wolf attacking the sheep!"

The cry echoed down the mountainside.

In the village, startled faces pressed against windows. Doors swung open. The blacksmith rushed from his forge, and the farmer trampled her cabbages in her haste. Everyone raced up the steep path to the meadow.

Together, they ran up to Rufus, huffing and puffing. "Where's the wolf?" they asked. Of course, there was no wolf to be seen. The meadow was full of drowsy sheep, and Rufus was rolling in the grass, laughing so hard he could barely speak.

"If you could only see your faces," he chortled.

"He's played a trick on us," the blacksmith grumbled, wiping the sweat from his forehead.

With that, the villagers trudged back down the path. Once again, the hours crawled by.

Rufus ate his lunch of bread and cheese, and then, as the sun climbed higher, he began to get bored again.

"What a wonderful prank that was," he thought. "How silly everyone looked. I wonder if I could fool them again."

With that, he jumped onto the same rock as before. "WOLF," he shouted. "WOOOOLF! Help! There's a great big wolf in the meadow!"

Again, windows and doors flew open in the village. People hurried into the street, raising the alarm. A little crowd of rescuers, led by the baker, raced up the path. Soon, they arrived in the meadow.

"Where's the wolf?" asked the baker, waving his rolling pin. "Are you hurt?"

Rufus looked at the baker's red face, smudged with flour, and laughed so hard, he fell off his rock. "I can't believe you fell for it *again*," he gasped. The farmer shook her long rake with disgust. "I've had enough of these games," she said angrily. "Let's all go home."

The grumbling villagers stomped back down the path. As Rufus watched them go, he wiped the tears of laughter from his eyes. "I'm sure they'll see the funny side some day," he said.

Now, the shadows were starting to lengthen

across the mountainside. It would soon be time for Rufus to gather up the flock of sheep and start for home.

But as he strolled through the meadow, the little shepherd spotted something strange moving at the edge of the forest. Beneath a leaning pine tree, one shadow seemed to lift up off the ground and glide out into the evening light.

A wolf!

It had dark, scruffy fur, pointed ears and yellow eyes. It also had a keen and hungry look, and was coming straight towards Rufus and the sheep.

Rufus's mind raced. The villagers weren't far away. If only they knew the danger he was in, they could easily come and rescue him.

"WOOOLF! HELP! HELP! WOOOOLF!"

So, for the third time that day, he shouted with all his might.

"WOOOLF! HELP! HELP! WOOOOLF!"

The shepherd boy's cry was so loud that it echoed off the farthest mountain peaks. The baker heard it, but he just kept kneading his dough. The farmer heard it, but she just kept weeding her garden. The blacksmith heard it too, over the ringing of his hammer. "I'm not falling for it this time," he muttered, as he thrust a red-hot horseshoe back into the fire.

Up in the meadow, Rufus waited in vain. Nothing stirred and nobody came. He shouted once more, but his cry just echoed in the valley. A few lights came on in the village.

"They don't believe me," Rufus realized. "They think it's just another trick. I wish I'd never told my stupid lie!"

The wolf was almost upon him. Rufus could see its teeth flashing, and with a terrible growl it sprang onto the nearest sheep.

Poor Rufus didn't wait to see what happened next. He dropped his shepherd's crook and bolted down the mountain path. He tumbled over rocks and scraped through brambles. At last, with his clothes torn and one shoe missing, Rufus reached the sleepy lanes of the village.

Although he was safe and sound, his flock was never seen again. Rufus was ashamed of what he'd done, and from then on, he was just a little more helpful and a little more kind. He helped the farmer with her weeding, and chopped wood for the baker's oven. He carried heavy iron to and from the blacksmith's forge – and in all the rest of his days, he was never naughty again.

Well, maybe just once or twice...

Stone Soup

It was a cold evening when a shabby-looking man in tattered clothes arrived at a cottage in some woods. The trees had almost lost all of their leaves, and the cold wind hinted that a harsh winter was just around the corner. The man whistled to keep his spirits up, and dug his hands deep into his pockets to warm them.

His pockets contained all he owned, apart from the coat on his back: a ragged handkerchief, an apple core, which he was keeping as an emergency snack, and a smooth, round pebble. He'd been walking all day and he was cold and tired, but here was a brightly lit cottage that was sure to have a roaring fire inside. Perhaps luck was on his side tonight, after all. He knocked on the door. It opened just a crack.

"What do you want?" a sharp voice demanded from inside the cottage.

"Er, good evening, madam, I wonder if I could trouble you with..."

"No you can't," the cross voice interrupted.

"I've got nothing for you. Go away!"

Of all the cottages in all the woods, he seemed to have found the one with the worst-tempered old woman. But he was not going to be put off quite so easily.

"I don't wish to be any trouble, madam, but I haven't eaten all day. All I ask is that you let me warm my hands by your fire and share some food."

The woman snorted. "Ha. *I* haven't eaten for *three days*! Times are hard around here, you know. There's no food to spare. So go away."

"Oh you poor dear woman," said the man, shaking his head, and inserting his foot into the crack of the door. "Three days! Goodness me. But, my dear lady, I was not suggesting that I share *your* food. I have in my pocket the single most important ingredient for a very fine soup."

The door opened a little wider.

"A soup so fine it is fit for kings," the man continued. "And what could be better than a nice, hot, steaming bowl of soup on such a chilly autumn night as this?"

The woman snorted again. "Soup fit for kings? Get away with you." But the door opened wider still, so that the man could see the woman's wrinkled old face. Her eyes peered distrustfully over a pair of round, wire-framed glasses.

"It's true, madam, although it might seem surprising. This here..." He dug his hand into his right pocket and with a flourish produced the pebble. "This pebble will produce a wonderful, nourishing and, dare I say, *superior* soup. All I need is for your gracious self to lend me a pot, and tell me where the well is, so that I can draw some water to fill it."

"Well, I'm not sure." The door opened further. The woman was so bent over the only thing keeping her upright must surely have been her stick.

"Just a pot, some water and some fire, madam, and I assure you we will both end the evening with full bellies and happy hearts."

The woman hesitated for a moment, then snapped, "Oh all right then. My second best cooking pot is there." (She wasn't going to trust her *best* pot to him.)

The door flung open with surprising force to reveal a snug-looking, warm room with a big black pot in one corner. "And the well is over there," she said, waving in the direction of the hen house. "Make it quick though! I don't want to let the heat out."

The man did as he was told, as quickly as he could. After all, the evening wasn't getting any warmer, and he wasn't getting any less hungry.

Once inside, with the pot on to boil, he took the shiny pebble out of his pocket again, and held it up to the light.

"It doesn't *look* like much," the woman sneered. "And whoever heard of stone soup anyway?" It was clear that she was beginning to have her doubts again, so the man – with another flourish – tossed the pebble into the air, caught it and dropped it into the boiling water.

"Stone soup, my dear madam, is a little known, nay, *secret* delicacy that not only tastes absolutely delicious, but is also highly nutritious. You should prepare your taste buds to be delighted, your stomach to be in heaven, your..."

"Will it take long?" she interrupted.

"Er, no, no, no. Not that long at all, madam. In fact, I can see it is already very nearly done. Could you lend me a spoon so that I might taste it?"

The old woman handed him a ladle.

"Mmmmm, not bad," declared the man,

after taking a sip. The
woman reached out to take
the ladle from him, but he
whisked it away from her,
and tipped its contents
back into the pot.

"Not bad at all, but not
quite there yet. I am sure, though, it would be
so much better with a little seasoning. I don't
suppose you have a bit of salt to spare do
you? That would really perk it up."

The woman shrugged. She could spare
a little salt couldn't she? Not that it would
make *soup from a stone* (she snorted) taste any
better, but a little salt was neither here nor
there. So she hobbled off to fetch a salt shaker
from her table.

The man added a generous amount, then tasted the soup again. "Yes. Yes! It's coming along nicely now. But I still think it could do with a little something. But what, I wonder? Um, let me see. Oh, I know! It would be so much better with some potato in it. I don't suppose...?"

"A potato," the woman grumbled. "Yes, I *suppose* I might have a potato somewhere."

The old woman shuffled off to a dark corner of the cottage and grabbed a couple of potatoes from a bulging sack. "I hope it's going to be worth it," she added as she handed them over. "I'll be annoyed if you waste them."

The man quickly cut the potatoes into chunks with a knife, and tossed them into the pot.

Not long after, he tasted the soup again. "Ah yes. *Now* we are getting there. But although it is, if I say so myself, already fit for a lord, it's not *quite* ready for a king yet. I don't suppose you have an onion do you?"

"An onion, he says. An *onion*! All right, he can *have* an onion," she muttered, as she went to get one from one of several strings of onions that were hanging by the sink.

But in spite of her apparent bad temper, she couldn't help feeling more and more curious about how this 'stone soup' was going to turn out.

When the man had chopped the onion and added it to the pot, even *she* had to admit that the soup was beginning to smell really rather good.

Stone Soup

The soup was beginning to smell really rather good.

"Yes, definitely getting there," the man said after another taste. "But, oh, I don't know..." He frowned. "It's a little thinner than I would have liked. I have been using this stone on and off for seven days now, after all. I mean, don't get me wrong. It's fine as it is. In some countries they judge a soup to be superior when it's this thin, but, well, I can't help thinking that a little barley would improve it *hugely*."

The woman gave him a hard stare – she wasn't going to let him know how eager she was to taste the soup now – and went off to fetch a bowl of barley from an almost-full barrel at the back of the kitchen.

"Mmmmmmm," the man said, as he took his next slurp of soup. "*Now* we're cooking.

But you know, I really do think..."

"Yes?"

"I really do think it would be so much better, so much more *kingly*, if..."

"Yes? If what?"

"Well, if there were a bit of meat we could put in it. It's such a pity there is none. Ah well." He sighed.

The woman sighed too. Salt, potato, onion, barley and now meat! He was asking a lot. But she supposed it was all in a good cause – if it improved the taste of the stone soup.

"All right," she said "I'll see what I can do. I might have a bit of something I was keeping for Sunday."

She cut a slab of meat from a huge joint that she was keeping on a shelf in her pantry, and brought it back to the man.

In the meat went. The smell was *unbelievably* good now and, after the man had taken another mouthful, he declared it ready.

"Fit for a king, madam," he announced. "*Or* a queen," he added, bowing. The old woman giggled and blushed like a young girl.

"Well in that case," she said, "we should eat it at the table!"

She brought her best bowls and spoons, together with a loaf of bread and a large slab of butter. Finally, she set a bottle of sweet, fresh apple juice on the table.

The soup was just as delicious as it smelled, and for a while the old woman seemed unable to speak. Then, with a huge smile on her face, she declared, "My goodness, this really is the best soup I have ever tasted. And to think it was made from a stone. Thank you so very much."

The man smiled and nodded. "It was a pleasure, madam."

He looked around the cottage at all the things the old woman hadn't wanted to share. "But in fairness, I cannot take all the credit. Really it was all the things *you* added that made the difference."

Tam Lin

Thud, thud, thud went the horse's hooves, as Tam Lin and his milkwhite steed came over the green hill. Tam was handsome and dashing and rode like the wind, but he'd been out hunting all day and had lost his way. Night was coming in and there was no moon to guide him.

In the twisting darkness, Tam's horse stumbled and he flew from the saddle with a cry.

For a moment, he lay there, dazed, then all at once he heard a whispering sound. He looked up and saw the Queen of the Fairies, glowing in the dark night.

"Did you know you were crossing Fairy Land?" she asked. "Did you know this green hill is my home?" Then she laughed. She had taken one look at the dashing Tam Lin and decided to make him her knight. "Now," she told him, "you belong to me. You no longer live in the world of men but are one of my Elven Company."

From that hour, Tam Lin guarded the forest, demanding trinkets and nuggets of gold from whoever passed his way. By night, he slept in the Fairy Queen's home, deep in the folds of the hill.

Seven years passed until, one spring, a woman named Janet came over the fairy hill. She had wild blonde hair and a skip in her stride and her skirt hitched up to her knees.

As she ran through the trees she saw a milkwhite steed tied up beside a well. Around the well climbed wild roses, nodding on their thin green stems. She picked a rose and smelled its sweet scent, and out sprang Tam Lin: "Who dares to come to the fairy forest? Who dares to come without my consent?"

"I dare," said Janet, standing tall and bold, flashing her golden hair. "And who are you to stop me?" she said, brave despite her fear.

"This is Fairy Land," Tam Lin replied. "It belongs to the Fairy Queen. If you want to pass through, you must pay me in gold, or pay me by other means." But as Tam Lin looked at Janet, he was filled with the urge to be free. "I belong to the Fairy Queen, so I cannot leave. But perhaps you could stay with me?"

Janet shook her golden head. She was wise to the fairy ways. "If I stay with you and live in the green hill, I'll be trapped forever in Fairy Land. I'll be trapped against my will."

So she picked up her moss-green skirt and turned on her heel instead. "I'm going back home to my father. I'm going back to the life I know." And away she went.

The months passed and the wind turned cold and the leaves blew down from the trees. But Janet still remembered the man she had met in the fairy forest and she longed to see him again. So one blustery day, she made her way, over the green hill, to the milkwhite steed by the well. She picked a wild rose and Tam Lin appeared again. "Who dares to come to the fairy forest without Tam Lin's consent?"

"I dare," said Janet. "I've come to hear your tale. Are you a man, or one of the fairy folk?"

Tam Lin told her of his human past, and his life among the fairies. "I long to escape," he said, "and tonight is my chance to be free. At midnight the fairy folk will ride past the well. Will you win me back from the Fairy Queen?"

Janet stood tall and bold, and though she felt afraid, she promised him, "I will."

"Then first," said Tam Lin, "you must let the black horse pass, and then the brown. Then quickly run to the milkwhite steed and pull the rider down. For he shall be none other than me, your Tam Lin."

"I'll do it," said Janet. "For you I'll face the Fairy Queen and her Elven Company."

But Tam Lin had more to tell. "The fairies will work their magic, to cast spell after spell after spell. I'll turn into a toad, a snake, a bear, a lion, a red hot iron and then a burning coal. On the last, you must throw me into the well. Only then will I be free and turn into a man again. Then cover me with your soft grey shawl and hide me out of sight."

And Janet did just as she was told. That night, she waited by the well in the gathering gloom, until the moon hung high, and at last she heard the sound of golden bells... the sound of fairy folk.

The first to pass was the black horse, and

Tam Lin

The fairies will work their magic, to cast spell after spell after spell.

she let the black horse go. The second to pass was the brown horse, and she let the brown horse go. Then came the rider on the milkwhite steed. Janet ran out from her hiding place. She ran for the rider and she pulled him down. Around her the fairies cast spell after spell after spell.

Tam Lin turned from toad to snake to bear to lion to red hot iron, and Janet held on still. She felt slimy scales and thick rough fur, but still she held on tight. Then, when her hands gripped a burning coal she ran with it, and though it scalded her she held it until she reached the well.

Janet threw the coal into the water, and in a flash, back came Tam Lin. She pulled him from the water and covered him with her shawl. Then she hid him beneath some branches, safely out of sight. She heard the Fairy Queen, calling out into the night.

"Who dares take away my bonniest knight? You have taken away my heart's delight. Had I known Tam Lin would go, I'd have taken out his heart of flesh, and put in a heart of stone."

But midnight passed and the riders had to go. The fairy folk passed by and Tam Lin was free at last.

Tam took Janet by the hand. They walked over the green hill. They went back to her village and they live there still, for never again would either of them step foot in Fairy Land.

The Bremen Town Musicians

The farmer was stomping around the farmyard grumbling again. "Useless old donkey. I could carry this load faster than you do!"

This wasn't true, of course. The donkey's load was far too heavy for the farmer. But the donkey was old, and he was tired, and, he had to admit, a lot less strong than he had been in his youth.

The donkey knew that if he couldn't work, then the farmer could not afford to keep him. There was only one thing left to do.

He would have to leave.

So that night, he chewed through his tether, kicked backwards with his hooves to break down the fence, and trotted down the lane, away from the farm forever.

"My legs may sometimes feel weak, and my body weary," he thought, "but I still have a fine, strong braying voice. I will go to the town of Bremen, famous for its musicians, and earn my keep making music."

He trotted most of the night to get as far away from the farm as possible, only pausing to nibble a blade of grass here and there, when he felt hungry. Early the next morning, he came across a dog lying panting on the roadside.

"Are you all right?" the donkey asked,
wondering why the
dog would look so
tired and out of
breath at this time
of the morning.

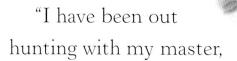

"I have been out
hunting with my master,
but I couldn't keep up," the dog gasped. "I am
just too old for this sort of thing. My master
will be furious when he discovers that I've
paused for a rest, but I really couldn't keep
going." The dog groaned. "He'll want to get
rid of me now."

The donkey nodded sympathetically. "It's a
terrible thing," he said. "We work hard for our

masters all our lives, and then, when we are ready for retirement, they just want to get rid of us."

The dog sighed, and looked as if he were about to start howling.

"I tell you what, my friend," the donkey continued hurriedly. "Why don't you come with me? I'm off to the town of Bremen to become a musician. We could form a band and make music there together."

The dog's ears pricked up when he heard this, and he quickly agreed to the donkey's suggestion.

They had not gone much further when they heard a pitiful mewling noise. There by the side of the road was a small black cat.

"What on Earth's the matter?" asked the dog.

"My life is over," mewed the cat. "I'm too tired and old to be out all night catching mice as my mistress wants me to. She calls me lazy and throws me outside when I try to settle down for the night for a snooze by the fire."

She sighed and licked her paw forlornly. "Is it really too much at my time of life to want to have a little nap at the end of the day, I ask you? You'd think I'd get *some* gratitude for all the mice I've caught over the years. But no. I heard her telling the master the other night that if I don't catch more mice, she's going to get rid of me."

"Oh poor Cat," said the donkey. "Why don't you come to Bremen with us? We are off to form a band. With your fine voice, you could join us."

"Why, thank you," the cat said, brightening up. "I'd *love* to come."

So the three animals set off down the road. It was almost dusk when they reached another farm. There, a rooster perched on top of a hen house was crowing with all his might.

The three animals stared up in astonishment.

"Why are you crowing at this time of day, Rooster?" the cat asked.

The rooster stopped crowing and looked down at the other animals. "I am crowing," he replied in a sad, but dignified manner, "because today is my last day. So I am doing what I love to do best."

He paused for a moment, to let out a deafening **cock a doodle doo**. "Tomorrow the farmer's wife is going to kill me and make me into soup," he continued. "She says I'm too old to be of any use and she might as well eat me."

"That's *terrible*," the others said together.

"You must come away with us," added the donkey. "We are off to Bremen to become musicians. Even without your fine voice you would be welcome to join us, but with a talent like yours, we could make a fortune."

So the rooster flapped down from his perch and the four of them hurried off in the direction of Bremen.

It was dark by now and the animals were feeling tired and hungry. They decided to leave the road to find shelter in some woods. The dog, the donkey and the cat settled down under a tree to sleep, and the rooster flew up into the branches where he felt safest. While he was up there, he spotted a light shining in the distance.

"I think there may be a cottage over there," he said, flying back down to the others. "Maybe there will be some food for us, or a warm fire for you, Cat, and you, Dog, to curl up next to."

"Mmm. And maybe some cream," said the cat, who was prone to wishful thinking. "Let's go and look."

They all agreed and set off towards the light.

There was indeed a cottage there, in a little

clearing. What they didn't know was that the cottage belonged to a gang of robbers.

The donkey trotted up to an open window, and peeked inside.

"Well, what can you see?" asked the little cat eagerly.

"There's a group of mean-looking men crowded around a table," replied the donkey. "Mmm. The table's just groaning with delicious-looking food and drink, including a whole jug of cream. And they're surrounded by lots of jewels and piles of money."

"Must be robbers," said the dog knowledgeably. "But I like the sound of the food. How can we get in there?"

The animals whispered for a moment and came up with a plan. The donkey positioned himself under the window, with his front hooves on the windowsill. Then the dog climbed onto the donkey's back.

"Ow! Watch your claws," growled the dog, as the cat clambered up on *his* back, and rested her paws on his shoulders.

"Ooh sorry," she purred, and then meowed as the rooster landed on her head.

"Ready?" asked the donkey.

"Woof!" barked the dog quietly.

"Meow," mewed the cat softly.

"Squawk!" squawked the rooster, perhaps a little more loudly than he should have.

"OK then. A one, and a two, and a three... SING!"

And the donkey brayed and the dog howled and the cat yowled and the rooster let out an

A one, and a two, and a three... SING!

eardrum-bursting "Cock a doodle doo!" all at the top of their voices.

The robbers were terrified. "Arggh! A four-headed monster is attacking us!" shrieked one, and they all fled from the cottage.

Some time later, the animals had finished the best meal they had ever eaten. They decided to put out the lights so they could go to sleep. After all, it had been a very tiring day.

The cat curled up by the dying fire. The dog settled on a comfy mat behind the door. The rooster flew up onto a beam near the ceiling, and the donkey made his way outside to sink down in a heap of clean, dry straw.

Meanwhile in the forest, the robbers were beginning to feel a little foolish. They hadn't even looked properly to see what had burst into their cottage. A four-headed monster? There was no such thing!

"What a coward you are," said one, prodding another. "Why don't you go back and have a look?"

"Me! Why *me*? Why not *him*?" said the other pointing to a third. This went on for a while until at last one of them agreed to go back and look.

The robber tiptoed up to the cottage, careful not to step on any telltale branches. He carefully opened the door praying that it wouldn't creak.

It was so dark inside that he stubbed his toe on the table, waking up the cat. Seeing the cat's eyes glowing in the dark, the robber thought that they were embers in the fireplace. He moved towards them, crouching down to light a match.

Not surprisingly, the cat was not very happy about being poked in the eye. She lashed out with her claws, hissing, spitting and scratching. The robber jumped up in terror and fell backwards over the dog, who bit him on the leg.

Crying out in pain, the man stumbled blindly into the yard, where the donkey kicked him with his hooves.

By now the rooster had woken up too and swooped down on the robber, clawing him with his feet and pecking with his beak, screaming "Cock a doodle doo!" in what seemed to the robber to be a blood-curdling way.

The robber fled from the cottage yard in terror, sobbing and screaming until he got back to his friends.

"There's... there's an evil, powerful witch in there," he managed to say in between big gulps of air. "Awful it was, just *awful*."

He shuddered. "She spat at me and scratched me with hideous, long, bony fingers. And she had an accomplice. A huge, hairy man who stabbed me with a knife, and *then* when I ran out into the yard, a massive monster beat me with a club, and a beast with wings called out 'There's the thief! There's the thief! Take him away!' before it flew down and attacked me. But I managed to fight them all off," he lied, puffing his chest up. "But only just, and maybe we shouldn't go back there…"

The robbers didn't need much convincing. They took off, leaving the cottage and the forest behind, never to return again.

And the animals, well, they were so happy in their new home – with enough money to buy all the food they could ever want for the rest of their lives – that they never made it to Bremen. But, every now and then, they would sit outside the house and sing a selection of songs, just in case they ever needed to perform them...

The Enormous Turnip

It had been a bad year for potatoes and a bad year for parsnips. The radishes were wrinkled and the carrots were spindly. Mr. and Mrs. Sprout the farmers had never had such bad luck.

"If this carries on, we won't have enough to eat," said Mr. Sprout.

"There are still the turnips..." Mrs. Sprout replied hopefully.

Every day, Mr. and Mrs. Sprout carefully weeded and watered the turnip field, and every night, they dreamed of turnips.

"Turnip soup," murmured Mr. Sprout.

"Turnips on toast," whispered Mrs. Sprout. "That turnip field is our final hope."

One morning, Mr. Sprout was cleaning his boots on the porch, when he spotted Mrs. Sprout sprinting down the path towards the farmhouse.

"You'll never believe this," she yelled. "Come and see!"

Mr. Sprout pulled on his boots as quickly

as he could and rushed after his wife. They kept running all the way to the turnip field.

There, the sight of something made Mr. Sprout stop in his tracks. "It's huge..." he whispered.

In the middle of the field, one turnip towered over all the rest. Its dark green leaves were taller than the hedgerow, and its purple top which poked above the soil was wider than a tractor's wheel.

"It's not just huge, it's ENORMOUS," said Mrs. Sprout. "And it's ready to be picked."

Mr. Sprout squared up to the enormous turnip and grabbed hold of the leaves.

"Pull!" said Mrs. Sprout.

Mr. Sprout pulled and pulled but the enormous turnip didn't move at all. It was

The Enormous Turnip

Mr. Sprout pulled and pulled but the enormous turnip didn't move at all.

firmly stuck in the ground.

"I'll help," said Mrs. Sprout. She gripped her husband by the waist, and dug her boots into the mud to steady herself.

"Pull!" said Mr. Sprout.

Together, they pulled and pulled with all their strength, but still the enormous turnip didn't move.

"Come help!" yelled Mr. Sprout to the farm boy, who was passing by.

"We'll pull that up easily," the farm boy said, flexing his muscles.

Mr. Sprout grabbed hold of the turnip's leaves again. Mrs. Sprout gripped Mr. Sprout's waist, and the farm boy grasped hers.

"Pull!" said Mr. Sprout.

The three of them pulled and pulled, but

the turnip didn't move. It didn't want to go anywhere.

"What next?" said the farm boy, who was bright red in the face from all the effort.

"Come and help us!" Mr. Sprout called to the farm dog.

Mr. Sprout grabbed the turnip. Mrs. Sprout gripped Mr. Sprout. The farm boy grasped Mrs. Sprout. The dog clenched the boy's coat between his teeth and sank his paws into the ground, ready to pull.

"Pull!" said Mr. Sprout.

They pulled and pulled until they were all out of breath. But the enormous turnip still didn't move.

Everyone was exhausted.

"What next?" Mr. Sprout gasped.

The farm dog bounded off and came back with the farm cat.

"Come help!" said Mr. Sprout.

The cat clutched the dog, who was biting the farm boy's coat, who was grasping Mrs. Sprout, who was gripping Mr. Sprout, who was grabbing the turnip.

"Pull!" said Mr. Sprout.

They pulled and pulled. But *still* the turnip didn't move.

A tiny mouse was fast asleep. She'd built her nest beside the enormous turnip. Its big leaves shaded her from the sun. But all the commotion woke her up.

Mrs. Sprout spotted her first. "Come help!" she said.

The mouse was in a helpful mood. She went to the back of the line and held onto the cat's tail. The cat was so tired from all the pulling, she didn't even mind.

"Pull!" said Mr. Sprout.

"Pull!" said Mrs. Sprout.

"Pull!" said the boy.

"Woof!" said the dog.

"Meow!" said the cat.

"Squeeeeak," said the mouse, and she pulled and pulled with all her might.

Deep under the ground, there was a rumbling, ripping sound as the roots of the enormous turnip loosened their grip on the earth. The turnip shuddered and shook.

"Keep pulling!" yelled Mr. Sprout. "We're almost there!"

Slowly but surely, the turnip was moving. Then, with an enormous **POP**, it burst out of the soil.

The mouse tumbled to the ground. The cat, the dog, the boy and the farmers tumbled after her.

Groaning and panting, they got to their feet. The enormous turnip lay on the soil, quite oblivious to the trouble it had caused.

Mrs. Sprout shook the soil from her boots. Mr. Sprout stood, speechless, staring at the vast vegetable lying in the field.

Finally he spoke. "Who's coming for dinner?" he said. "I hope you like turnip."

The Fisherman and the Genie

There was once a fisherman who was very unlucky in his job. Although he worked hard, he rarely seemed to catch enough fish to feed his family.

Every morning, he went down to the sea and flung his nets out onto the water, but in the last week he hadn't caught anything other than an old boot.

"This morning, my luck will turn," he said to himself, as he set out so early that the moon was still visible.

He didn't really believe it, so he was amazed when, not long after he'd thrown his nets out onto the water, he felt a sharp tug. His heart beat fast as he hauled the nets in. They felt heavy, but all he'd caught was an old cart wheel.

The fisherman sighed. "Typical. It's broken the nets in several places too," he grumbled. He mended the nets and flung them back into the sea.

A short while later, he felt another tug.

'A huge haul of fish,' he thought.

'This time it *has* to be!' But when he pulled the nets in, they were full of nothing but old broken pots.

The third time, after he had caught a net full of stones, he was almost ready to give up. But he thought of his wife and children: "One more try," he told himself. "Just one more try."

This time, when he drew the nets in, they contained only one thing. One small, but very heavy thing. A plain copper bottle with a stopper in the top, and sealed with lead.

"Well it's not much to look at, and I can't eat it," he muttered, "but perhaps I can sell it. I should get enough money to feed my family for at least a day or two."

Looking at the bottle closely, he began to wonder if there might be something of value inside. After all, someone had gone to a lot of trouble to seal it, and it felt heavier than you might expect from such a small bottle.

He shook it, but it didn't sound as if there was anything inside. Digging a knife out of his pocket, he sliced off the seal, popped open the stopper and peered in. He couldn't see a thing, so he shook it upside down.

At first, nothing came out. Then suddenly, a plume of thick, white smoke began to pour out of the bottle. The fisherman dropped the bottle in surprise, but the smoke continued to flow out, billowing upwards and spreading out until it seemed to fill the horizon.

Gradually, the smoke began to take shape. There, hovering before the fisherman, was a huge genie.

There, hovering before the fisherman, was a huge genie.

The fisherman was too frightened to move. The genie rose higher.

"Solomon, oh Solomon, great prophet," he began in a sorrowful voice. "I beg your forgiveness, I throw myself on your mercy. Never again, oh majestic, oh wondrous one, shall I disobey you."

The fisherman was so surprised that he forgot to be afraid. "Solomon?" he laughed. "*Solomon*! The old king? He's been dead for hundreds of years. What on Earth were you doing in that bottle?"

The genie looked down at the fisherman, and his expression changed from fear to anger. "*Who*," he said "are *you*? And how dare you speak to me so impolitely?"

The fisherman laughed again. "Oh, I *do* beg

your pardon," he said. "Oh magnificent genie," he added, mockingly, when he saw the genie's annoyed expression.

The genie huffed, and they glared at each other for a moment.

"So," the fisherman said, breaking the silence. "Do I get three wishes, then?"

The fisherman knew that when genies are released from bottles, they always grant three wishes to the person who set them free.

"I'll give you *one* wish," the genie replied, nostrils flaring.

The fisherman was a little disappointed, but one wish was better than none.

"Fantastic!" he said rubbing his hands together. "Well then, I'd like..."

"One wish," the genie interrupted, "which

is your choice of how you shall die."

"Wh...what?" The fisherman's jaw dropped. "Hang on a moment, I just set you free. What sort of reward is killing me supposed to be?"

The genie sighed impatiently and stared at the fisherman as if he were a fool. "Look," the genie said. "I've been stuck in this bottle for hundreds of years."

"Yes, exactly," began the fisherman, "which is why..."

"If someone had let me go during the first hundred years," the genie interrupted again, "I would have been so grateful that I'd have made them rich beyond their wildest dreams. I'd have made their children rich, and their children's children rich. But no one did."

"Yes, but..."

"So, for the next hundred years I was a little annoyed. But I was also getting more desperate, and I would have opened up all the treasures of the Earth and given them to anyone who released me."

"All right, so..."

"After three hundred years, I thought to myself, 'Right. If anyone releases me now, I will make them ruler of all the Earth. All of the universe, if he or she so wishes. And I will always be at their side granting them three wishes every single day. Three wishes, whatever they want. No quibbles, no conditions.' But did anyone release me? No. So by this point, I really was rather cross."

The genie, a frightening grin on his face, loomed down towards the fisherman.

"So, I made a vow to myself that I would kill whoever eventually released me. Without mercy. No arguing. Stone dead."

The genie rose up again and folded his arms as if to say, 'And what do you think of that?' "You wouldn't want me to break my promise to myself, would you?"

"Um, actually..." the fisherman began.

"So. How *would* you like to die?" the genie asked. "I can do explosions, disintegration, fatal diseases. Anything you want really.

Although I really would prefer it if it was something imaginative."

The fisherman could see that he was not going to change the genie's mind. He would have to think quickly if he wanted to get out of this alive.

"All right," he said. "I can see you are a genie of great resolve. But please at least would you do just one thing for me before I die? Answer me a question."

The genie scowled for a moment. "Well I suppose so," he replied, "but make it snappy. I can't float around here all day, you know. People to see, things to do."

"Well," the fisherman said, "what I'd like to know is, how could such a massive genie like you get into such a tiny bottle as this?"

The fisherman held up the bottle. "I mean, it's not very believable is it? In fact, I'm beginning to wonder if you were ever in this bottle in the first place. Perhaps it was just a trick of the light. Or maybe I just imagined it. I haven't had anything to eat this morning, after all."

"Of course I was in the bottle," the genie spluttered indignantly.

"I'm not sure I believe you."

"I was! I swear to it!"

"Uh uh. I don't believe you."

"All right!" the genie said. "I'll show you." And he dissolved into a plume of smoke, which poured back into the bottle.

As soon as the genie was inside, the fisherman popped the stopper back in.

"Ha! Now it's your turn to beg a wish from *me*, genie," he sneered.

There was
a brief silence.

"Fisherman," came
a wheedling voice.
"Please do not pay any
attention to what I said

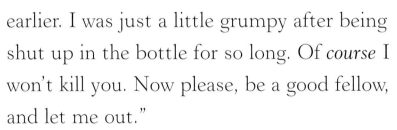

earlier. I was just a little grumpy after being shut up in the bottle for so long. Of *course* I won't kill you. Now please, be a good fellow, and let me out."

"Hmm... I'm not sure," said the fisherman, drumming his fingers on the bottle.

"I will make it worth your while," the genie said enticingly.

"Oh, I don't know, genie... I think that

maybe I should just throw this bottle back into the sea where it came from."

"Oh please no," wailed the genie. "Please, please, please, please let me out. I can see you are a kind man and wouldn't do anything so cruel."

"Nope," the fisherman said, and lifted the bottle up as if to throw it back into the sea.

"I will make you rich!"

The fisherman paused for a moment, as if he were giving the promise careful thought. Then...

"Oh, well all right," said the fisherman, and he pulled out the stopper.

Out the genie whooshed, a worrying grin on his face. "Don't worry. I am not going to kill you," he said, laughing at the fisherman's expression. "Here's what you have to do. Pick up your nets and come with me."

The genie grabbed the fisherman by the arm and they flew up into the air, past a town, over the mountains and down into a valley. They landed by a lake that lay between four hills.

"Now then, fisherman. Cast your net into the water."

The fisherman did as he was told. The lake was full of beautiful, shimmering fish of four different shades – white, red, blue and yellow – and the fisherman caught one of each.

"All right," the genie said. "Now take those fish to the Sultan. He will give you more money than you have ever seen in your life. You may do this once a day, but never more than once a day."

The fisherman shrugged and agreed. 'More money than he had ever seen' was good enough for him.

So the fisherman took the fish to the Sultan. The Sultan, intrigued by the unusual appearance of the fish, was delighted and paid the fisherman with bags of gold coins. The fisherman went home to his wife, happy and rich, and neither he nor his family ever went hungry again.

Chicken Licken

Chicken Licken ignored his mother all the time. He ignored her when she asked him to clean up. He ignored her when she said he should go to bed. He ignored her when she told him to have a bath.

Most of all, he ignored her when she warned him to be careful.

"Why can't I go outside?" Chicken Licken would cluck. "It's so boring in the farmyard."

Every time, his mother would reply, "A young chick faces all sorts of dangers beyond the fence. If you stay put, you'll stay safe."

One day, Chicken Licken decided he didn't want to stay put. He waited until his mother wasn't looking and then slipped away.

For the very first time, he left the farmyard. Everything felt new and exciting. He ran down hills. He climbed trees. He jumped in puddles.

All this exploring made Chicken Licken tired. When he came to a soft patch of moss, he lay down and fell asleep.

He slept soundly, until all at once he was woken up by a knock on the head. An acorn had fallen on him from the tree above.

"Owww," cried Chicken Licken, with a start. He looked up. He looked down. He looked all

around. He didn't see the
acorn. He didn't see
anything unusual.

"Oh dear, oh
dear," Chicken
Licken groaned.
"That never happened to me
in the farmyard. Whatever can it mean?"

He was very puzzled indeed. He sat down
and looked up. The answer came to him from
above. The sky must be falling!

The thought made Chicken Licken's
feathers shiver.

"What should I do? What should I do?"
he gabbled. "I don't have a clue what to do."

When he had calmed down, Chicken
Licken stopped to think more carefully about

his next step. This was very important news. Only someone very important would be able to help him.

"I need to tell the King!" he cried.

He had to get back to the farmyard as quickly as possible. He ran all the way, until he crashed into Henny Penny outside her coop.

"Whatever is the matter?" Henny Penny clucked, worriedly.

"The sky is falling!" Chicken Licken cried. "I'm going to tell the King."

Henny Penny didn't want to hang around the farmyard if the sky was falling. "I'll come with you," she squawked.

The two birds flapped past the barns and the hen house. They made a terrible noise outside Cocky Locky's pen.

"Whatever is the matter?" crowed Cocky Locky, angrily.

"The sky is falling!" Chicken Licken blurted impatiently.

"We're going to tell the King," piped Henny Penny, feeling very important.

Cocky Locky didn't want to be left out. "I'll come with you," he called.

The three birds charged onwards. They passed the pond, waving their wings in the air.

"Whatever is the matter?" quacked Ducky Lucky, with a splash.

"The sky is falling!" Chicken Licken panted.

"We're going to tell the King," added Cocky Locky. "At once."

"This sounds very serious," Ducky Lucky warbled. "I'll come with you."

The four birds ran away from the pond.
They passed Goosey Loosey who was napping
in her nest.

"Whatever is the matter?" Goosey Loosey
hissed as they charged past.

"The sky is falling!" Chicken Licken clucked.

"We're going to tell the King," piped up
Ducky Lucky.

"I'll come with you," honked Goosey Loosey,

who was now wide awake. She jumped out of her nest and followed the others.

The five birds ran out from the farmyard and into the woods. At the edge of the trees, they stumbled over Turkey Lurkey, who was out hunting for worms.

"Whatever is the matter with you all?" Turkey Lurkey gobbled.

"The sky is falling!" Chicken Licken cried.

"We're going to tell the King," explained Goosey Loosey.

"I'll come with you," Turkey Lurkey squawked. Then he paused to ask a simple question. "How do we get to the palace?"

Chicken Licken realized he didn't have a clue. Neither did Henny Penny, Cocky Locky, Ducky Lucky or Goosey Loosey.

All six birds went into a blind panic. They flittered and fluttered in every direction, flapping and flailing, squalling and squawking.

Eventually this dreadful noise attracted the attention of Foxy Loxy.

Foxy Loxy was hungry. He had been prowling around the tall farmyard fences for weeks. When he came across these six silly birds, he knew he might finally have a chance to feed his family. But he would have to be very clever and very sly.

"Whatever is the matter?" Foxy Loxy asked in a soft, gentle voice.

"The sky is falling!" Chicken Licken trilled.

"We're going to tell the King," gabbled Turkey Lurkey. "But we don't know the way to the palace!"

Chicken Licken

Eventually this dreadful noise attracted the attention of Foxy Loxy.

Foxy Loxy said he knew the way. "There's a shortcut down this dark path," he added. "Quick. We don't have a minute to spare."

The birds raced after Foxy Loxy, straight up to his burrow door. "The palace is just through here," he said, licking his lips.

In walked Chicken Licken, followed by Henny Penny, Cocky Locky, Ducky Lucky, Goosey Loosey and Turkey Lurkey. Foxy Loxy followed them in and closed the door...

That evening, Foxy Loxy and his family enjoyed the best dinner of their lives. They ate under a sky full of stars.

"Daddy, how did you trick those silly birds?" asked the cubs.

"They tricked themselves," said Foxy Loxy. "I can hardly be blamed if they didn't keep their wits about them, the foolish creatures. Whoever heard of the sky falling?"

At that moment, something fell from a tree. It hit Foxy Loxy right on the top of his head. He didn't see that it was an acorn.

He looked up. He looked down. He looked all around. A long shadow fell over his face.

"Maybe I've been too hasty," he said in a slow, deep growl. "Maybe Chicken Licken was right all along... Does anybody know the way to the palace? I've got something I need to tell the King."

The Little Nut Tree

Tommy Tuck was poor. He was so poor he only had three possessions: a little hut, a little bed and a little garden. In his garden, there was only one tree: a little nut tree, with spindly branches and a thin trunk. It didn't grow any nuts. It didn't even grow any leaves.

One winter, the wind was even colder and stronger than usual. The little nut tree shivered and shook. Inside his hut, Tommy shivered and shook too. He was too poor to afford wood for a fire, so he sat in his bed with the covers pulled up around his ears to keep warm. But he was still cold.

When the snow began to fall, Tommy grew even colder. Outside, the little nut tree glistened with frost.

"I should turn that old tree into firewood," said Tommy to himself. "It's no good for anything else. I can't even sell nuts at the market, because it never grows any."

But no matter how cold he was, Tommy couldn't bring himself to cut down the little nut tree.

"I remember when that
tree was just a nut in
the ground," he said
stubbornly. "I watered it
and cared for it, and I'm
going to stick with it."

Then he added:
"However spindly and useless it is."

At last, the snow melted, and spring came.
The sun shone, but still the little nut tree
didn't grow any leaves, or any nuts. Tommy
was so poor he had to sell his little bed. But
he wouldn't sell his beloved nut tree.

One morning, Tommy woke up and went to
the window to stretch. He was aching all over
from sleeping on the floor. Then he spotted
something out of the window. Something

was growing, right there on one of the tree's spindly branches.

"I don't believe it!" Tommy yelled.

Forgetting about his aches and pains, he rushed into the garden in his nightshirt. Sure enough, there was something hanging from a branch, which just yesterday had been bare. But it wasn't a nut. It was too big to be a nut.

Tommy stared in astonishment. It looked like a type of fruit called a nutmeg, but not like any nutmeg Tommy had seen at the market. It was made of...

"Pure silver," Tommy gasped.

A bird sang overhead and Tommy looked up. There among the branches, something else was glittering. This was even bigger than the nutmeg. A golden pear.

There among the branches, something else was glittering.

Tommy felt weak. He'd never even dreamed of such riches and yet here they were in his garden. The nut tree, which had never even grown a leaf before, had grown this incredible magical fruit.

Soon, news spread of the magical tree in Tommy Tuck's garden. A rich merchant came to see Tommy.

"I want to buy your nut tree," he announced. "I'll pay you twenty silver coins."

Tommy knew that twenty silver coins would be enough to keep his hut warm all through the winter, but he refused. He'd loved his little tree ever since it was a sapling. It belonged with him, and he couldn't bear the thought of someone taking it away. The rich merchant scratched his head and left.

Then a wealthy duke came to visit Tommy.

"Sell me your nut tree," he demanded. "I'll pay you fifty gold coins."

Fifty gold coins would be enough to buy a large house with a huge garden full of nut trees. He'd never be cold or hungry or uncomfortable again, but still Tommy refused.

So Tommy stayed in his hut and slept on the floor. But the sight of the silver nutmeg and the golden pear shining in the sun each morning kept his spirits up, and his body no longer ached.

Even the little nut tree stopped looking so spindly and frail. It stood tall and proud and didn't let the wind blow it around.

Meanwhile, the news of Tommy's little nut tree had spread across the sea. In Spain, the

King's daughter, Princess Sofia, was sat on her enormous bed piled high with downy pillows when she heard the news. She was fascinated by the boy who refused to sell his magical tree, even though he was so poor. All the boys Princess Sofia knew were preening princes, who didn't love anything apart from looking at themselves in the mirror. She was determined to meet Tommy, and to see the little nut tree he loved so much.

"I won't allow it. You're not going all that way by yourself," the King said.

"Yes I am," said the Princess. She was just as stubborn as Tommy.

Tommy was in his garden watering the little nut tree, when he heard a grand procession in the distance. A messenger ran up to him.

"Prepare for the arrival of Princess Sofia!" he announced, as grandly as he could for someone who was so out of breath.

Tommy dropped his watering can in shock. A princess? Coming to see him? He'd never even *seen* a princess before, let alone had to talk to one.

He was even more nervous when he saw Princess Sofia's coach. Its huge shiny wheels were almost taller than his hut, and it was drawn by six white horses.

The door swung open and, as the Princess climbed down the steps, Tommy couldn't help but stare. Her dress was made of crimson silk and the hair cascading down her back was jet black. She was the most beautiful person Tommy had ever seen.

The Princess grinned. "Are you Tommy?"
she asked. "Do you mind if I take a look at
your tree? I've heard all about it."

Tommy found he couldn't quite speak. He
merely led the Princess to the little tree. She
gazed up in wonder at its branches, admiring
the shining nutmeg and pear. But she also
noticed Tommy's threadbare shirt, and the big
holes in his shoes.

"What a wonderful tree," she said. "Don't you want to sell it? You'd never be poor again."

Tommy blushed. "I don't care much about being rich," he stuttered. "It sounds silly, but a little hut and my little nut tree are good enough for me."

"It's not silly at all," said the Princess sincerely. She'd never met anyone like Tommy. "It's your tree and you love it."

"I want you to have it," said Tommy. Then he turned bright red and added hastily, "Just to thank you for coming all this way."

Of all the expensive presents Princess Sofia had been offered, this was the most wonderful of them all.

"Oh no, I couldn't take your precious tree away," she replied.

"You should plant it in the palace gardens," said Tommy firmly. "Please will you accept it?"

The Princess looked at the tree, with its glinting golden pear and shiny silver nutmeg. It would make a wonderful addition to her palace gardens. But the palace no longer seemed such a wonderful place to the Princess.

"I don't want to live in a palace now I've met you. Would you mind if I lived here instead?" she said.

From somewhere, Tommy found enough courage to ask the Princess a question of his own. This time, she didn't refuse, and the very next day, they were married underneath the little nut tree.

Tommy and Princess Sofia lived together

in the little hut with the little garden for the rest of their lives. The Princess found that there was much more to life than being rich... although she did insist on buying a few new things for the hut.

The Ugly Duckling

"Will these eggs *never* hatch?" the mother duck quacked softly to herself. There was no one else around to hear her, and that was the problem. She didn't mind sitting on the eggs, but the place she'd chosen to make her nest – a safe place away from the hustle and bustle of the farmyard and the noisy splish-sploshing of the pond – was also a lonely place.

No one came to visit her and she was tired of sitting there all by herself.

Fortunately, she didn't have much longer to wait. One morning, just when the mother duck could feel the water calling her to go for a quick refreshing swim, she felt the tiniest movement and heard a muffled cracking sound.

Peering carefully under her wings, she saw a little beak popping out through the shell of an egg, and then another and another. Before she knew it, she had five fluffy, yellow ducklings staring wide-eyed at the huge world and making 'peep peep' noises.

"That's a fine brood you have there," an elderly duck quacked, as she waddled up the bank to the nest.

"Why thank you," replied the mother duck, standing up to stretch her legs, and flapping her wings in pride.

"What's *that?*" the old duck said, staring at the nest.

The mother duck looked down. "Oh yes. I'm still waiting for this one..."

There, in her nest, was one more

egg, bigger and a little paler than the others.

"It's a turkey egg!" declared the old duck. "Mark my words, it's a turkey egg. If I were you, I would just leave it there and go and teach your young ones to swim."

The mother duck wasn't so sure. "No, I've been sitting here for so long now, I might as well sit here a little while longer. I think I'll just wait and see what happens."

"Suit yourself," said the old duck, and waddled off to the pond, tutting and quacking disapprovingly as she went.

The mother duck didn't have much longer to wait. The very next day she heard the egg cracking beneath her. In no time at all, a little head appeared out of a hole in the large egg.

"**Parp parp**," it said. Not "**peep peep**" like her other ducklings. At last, her final baby was hatching out. But when the little bird emerged from its shell, she gasped. He was not cute and fluffy and yellow like the other ducklings, but big and dirty white and clumsy-looking.

He was, in fact, the ugliest duckling she had ever seen.

"Perhaps it *is* a turkey," the mother duck thought anxiously. "Ah well, I'll soon find out. Tomorrow I shall take them all to the pond."

The next morning, bright and early, the mother duck led her children down to the water. In the ducks splashed, one after another. For a heart-stopping moment, their bodies disappeared below the surface before they popped back up again, peeping contentedly.

The ugly duckling, she saw to her relief, enjoyed the water just as much as his brothers and sisters, and swam just as well too. "So he's *not* a turkey," she quacked happily.

Later that day, the mother duck decided

it was time to take the ducklings to meet
the other animals in the farmyard. The first
animal they had to meet was a grand old
Spanish duck. "Keep your feet turned out and
quack politely," the mother duck whispered to
them. "She's very important."

The Spanish duck peered down her beak
at the little family. "Not bad, not bad, I
suppose," she quacked haughtily, but then
she spotted the ugly duckling.

"*What* is *that*? So big and so very, *very* ugly." Her feathers ruffled. "We cannot have something like *that* in *my* farmyard." And the other animals quacked and hooted and cackled in agreement.

"But... but... He's just been in the egg too long," the mother duck stuttered. "And he swims nicely, and...and I'm sure he'll grow up to look like a normal duck."

But no one agreed with her. The other

ducks pecked him and a turkey flew at him, frightening the little duckling half to death. Sadly, the mother duck took her children back to her nest.

Things got even worse for the ugly duckling over the next few weeks. The ducks bit him, the chickens pecked him and the farmer's girl kicked him. His brothers and sisters began to pick on him, and even his mother started to say she wished she had never bothered to hatch him.

Lonely and miserable, he realized that the only thing he could do was leave.

So, one afternoon, he waddled away from the farm and made his way to a moor. There, he met some wild ducks.

"What sort of duck are you?" they quacked.

"You are so ugly." But they didn't drive him away, at least, so the duckling stayed, not sure where else to go.

Then, a couple of days later, some wild geese swooped down.

"My goodness you're a funny sort of duck, aren't you. Still we don't care that you're ugly. Why don't you come with us? We are flying off to another moor where the food is better."

The duckling was happy that they didn't turn him away. He was about to take off with them when there was a deafening noise: "BANG POP BANG!"

"It's the hunters!" the wild geese cried. Soon a hundred geese rose up into the air to escape the hunters' guns and the ferocious dogs that had come bounding up onto the moor.

The little duckling was so terrified that he couldn't fly, and just hid his head under his wing. He heard the sound of heavy breathing and felt hot breath on his body.

Peeking out from under his wing, he saw the massive mouth of a dog bearing down on him. Saliva dripping from the beast's teeth as it snarled. The duckling prepared himself for the worst, but the dog just ran off.

'I'm too ugly even for a dog to eat me,' thought the duckling sadly.

The duckling stayed there, hiding under his wing until all the hunters and their hounds had gone. Then he ran and ran as fast as he could through meadows and fields. A storm was brewing and, just when he thought he could run no more, he saw an old house.

Peeking out from under his wing, he saw the massive mouth of a dog...

The house was so decrepit that the door was off its hinges and he was able to crawl inside.

The cottage was owned by an old woman who lived there with a cat and a hen. The woman couldn't see very well, and thought that the duckling was a grown-up female duck. "Perhaps if I keep her we shall get some eggs," she muttered to herself, and so she allowed the duckling to stay.

But life in the cottage, although warm and dry, was not a happy one for the duckling. The cat and the hen teased him because he couldn't purr or lay eggs, and laughed at him when he said he longed to go for a swim.

"If you could learn to purr or lay eggs you wouldn't think of such ridiculous things," they said. "If you can't fit in, you might as well go."

So after a few weeks, the ugly duckling left. He found a lake to swim in, and there one morning, three beautiful white birds, birds more beautiful than anything he had ever seen, flew down onto the lake. Then, just a few moments later, they were off again, soaring up into the sky.

The duckling had no idea what type of bird they were, but he felt a strong longing to fly off and away with them. He flapped his wings, and let out a cry so strange that it alarmed him. But he knew it was no good. His wings weren't strong enough to fly far and, besides, why would these lovely birds allow such an ugly creature as him to fly with them? So he swam away unhappily, hoping to find some shelter from the chilly wind.

Winter was fast approaching. Gradually, the lake began to freeze up, and the duckling had to swim in circles to keep the water around him from freezing solid.

It was an especially cold and miserable winter that year. The duckling was beginning to think that it would never end when, one day, the sun seemed a little warmer, the birds sang a little more cheerfully and he noticed the trees were in blossom. Spring had arrived at last!

The ugly duckling heard a strange cry and the loud sound of wings whirring in the air.

When he looked up, he saw the beautiful white birds he had dreamed of since he first saw them months ago.

"I must go to them," he thought. "Even if they hate me because I am ugly, I must be with them. Even if it's the last thing I ever do."

The duckling flapped his wings and knew that this time they were strong enough take him up high and far away.

He soared on the breeze, following the white birds, until they came to rest on the large pond outside a big country house.

Landing on the water, the other birds turned and swam frighteningly fast straight for him. The duckling lowered his head, sure he was going to be attacked, expecting them to peck and bite him. But as he bent down, he caught sight of himself in the water. For a moment, he couldn't believe his eyes. He looked...he looked *just like them*.

He was white and had a long graceful neck and a lovely bright orange beak. And when the other birds reached him, they did not attack him, but stroked his neck with their beaks in greeting.

"Look! Look there's a new swan in the pond," he heard a child cry out at the edge of the water.

"He is so beautiful," another said. "Even more beautiful than the others!"

And the ugly duckling – now a beautiful swan – felt so happy that he didn't know what to do with himself and, at first, hid his head bashfully under his wing.

When he looked up and saw the other swans bowing their heads at him, he stretched out his neck into a graceful arch. He ruffled his beautiful white feathers as he joined them, swimming joyfully in the morning sunlight, no longer ashamed or afraid.

The Magic Porridge Pot

Far away and long ago, lived a little girl and her mother in a tumbledown cottage on a hill. There were woods above them and a village below them, and they were very happy together, but for one thing... They were so poor there was nothing to eat.

Every night, the little girl would go to bed with a tummy growling with hunger, and all night long she would dream and dream of food.

One day, the little girl was walking through the woods in search of berries to eat, when she met an old woman.

"I know you for a good little girl," said the old woman.

"Oh I am, I am," said the little girl.

"And I know you for a hungry little girl," said the old woman.

"Oh I am, I am," said the little girl. And she started to wonder if the old woman might be a witch to know so much about her.

The little girl was right. The old woman *was* a witch. Not a mean, nasty one, with long yellow teeth and a bag full of frogs, but a kind, *good* witch (for far away and long ago the world was full of kind, good witches).

"And because you are so hungry," the old woman went on, "I am giving you a magic pot. It means you will never, ever want for food again."

The little girl gasped, for no sooner had the old woman said the word 'pot' than a pot appeared in front of her.

"Is it really magic?" asked the little girl.

The old woman smiled. "Cook, little pot, cook!" she chanted, and all at once the pot began shaking and dancing. When the little girl looked inside, she could see it was bubbling with sweet-smelling porridge.

"Oh!" cried the little girl, clapping her hands together. "How delicious!"

The old woman waited until the pot was full to the brim and then, "Stop, little pot, stop!" she chanted. The pot stopped cooking and the famished little girl began eating.

"May I take it home?" she asked, as soon as she had finished.

"You may," said the old woman. "It is for you and your mother. Farewell, child."

And with a strange sort of "PLINK" she vanished.

The little girl ran home as fast as she could, dragging the pot behind her. She showed it to her mother and chanted, "Cook, little pot, cook!" just as the old woman had done, and sure enough it began cooking.

When there was porridge for two, the little girl said, "Stop, little pot, stop!" and sure enough, the pot stopped.

"We're saved!" cried her mother, and they danced around the room, and from that day on they never felt a moment's hunger again. Their tummies were always full of delicious, sweet-smelling porridge.

One day, the little girl set out for a walk, leaving her mother alone in the house. After a while, the mother began to feel hungry so she said, "Cook, little pot, cook!" and the little pot began to bubble with porridge. When it was full to the brim, she said, "Stop!"

But the pot didn't stop. It kept cooking and bubbling. Porridge spilled over the edge and went "SPLISH, SPLOSH, SPLASH!" all over the floor.

"Oh stop! Stop!" cried the mother again, but *still* the pot wouldn't stop. Now there was a great big pool of porridge on the floor and it was spreading fast.

"Oh dear, oh dear," said the mother, wringing her hands, for she knew she had forgotten how to make the pot stop. And the more she worried about it, the less she could think what the right words were.

"Please, stop!" she tried. And then, "Lovely little pot, if you could just do what I ask, and stop cooking, I'd be very grateful," and when that didn't work: "Stop this instant, little pot, or I'll give you what for."

But the pot *still* didn't stop. By now the pool of porridge was bubbling along the floor and heading out of the door.

"Stop, you HORRID pot!" shouted the mother at the top of her voice, and of course that didn't make the pot stop either. In fact, it cooked and bubbled more furiously than ever. The pool of porridge was now a thick, sludgy river that was glooping down the hill.

The mother ran after it, crying, "Stop! Stop!" and "Porridge Alert!" as the sludgy river of porridge became a terrible slurping torrent heading straight for the village below.

At the sound of the mother's cries, the villagers rushed out of their houses and looked in dismay at the torrent of porridge.

"Stop that porridge!" they shouted. But stopping porridge turned out to be a very tricky thing indeed. The porridge came in through their doors and oozed out of their

"We're being taken over by porridge!" wailed the villagers.

windows. In some cases, a great tide of porridge picked up whole houses and carried them away down the hill. Some people were swimming in porridge, and others were floating around in boats on top, but it was so thick and so gloopy no one could get away.

"We're being taken over by porridge!" wailed the villagers. "Is there no one who can help?"

Luckily, at that very moment, the little girl came back from her walk and quickly realized what was going on.

"Stop, little pot, stop!" she said, and, at long last, the pot stopped.

But as for the village... I'm afraid to say they are *still* eating porridge.

The Brave Little Tailor

O ne day, long, long ago, in a time of knights and giants, a little tailor sat working by the open window of his shop. He was sewing brass buttons on a new coat – but it was nearly lunch time and his eyes strayed to the loaf of bread and the pot of strawberry jam on his table.

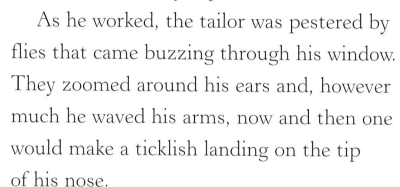

"Just three more buttons," he murmured to himself. "Or maybe just one more button."

As he worked, the tailor was pestered by flies that came buzzing through his window. They zoomed around his ears and, however much he waved his arms, now and then one would make a ticklish landing on the tip of his nose.

This was bad enough, but the flies soon discovered the pot of jam. When the hungry tailor saw them climbing around its sticky sides, he decided that enough was enough.

"I'll show you!" he cried. He swung the new coat through the air, brass buttons and all, and struck a mighty blow across the table. The jam tipped over, the loaf tumbled onto the floor, and a handful of flies were left dead on their backs, with their jam-covered feet in the air.

The little tailor counted them with pride.

"One, two, three, four, five, six, seven! Well, it's not every day that a man kills seven with one blow."

In fact, the tailor was so pleased with this achievement that he celebrated by making himself a handsome green sash. Across it, in large letters of golden thread, he embroidered these words: SEVEN WITH ONE BLOW.

The sash fit him perfectly. When he saw how dashing he looked in his little shop mirror, the tailor came to a decision.

"The town – no – *all the world* will hear of this," he announced. He thrust his scissors into his belt and threw a sack of provisions over his shoulder.

He looked around once more at his old workshop, but it now seemed small, stale and ordinary. And so, with the new sash glittering on his chest, he set out into the wide world to make a name for himself.

The little tailor walked boldly through fields and farms and into the forest. At last, he came to a great hill and at the summit he found a giant sitting and staring lazily across the countryside. The giant had finished his midday meal, and was using a small pine tree as a toothpick.

"Hello, friend," the tailor called. "Isn't this lovely weather for two free and easy fellows like us?"

The giant burped rudely – a sound that could be heard three counties away – and leaned over to examine the little tailor.

"*Fellows like us*? Do you dare to compare yourself to me, you miserable flea?"

"Oho!" cried the tailor, tapping his sash. "You should think twice about insulting a man like myself."

Taken aback, the giant peered at the golden letters glittering far below.

"Seven with one blow," he thought. "Did this creature really kill seven men with just one blow? Maybe I should have been more polite.

Maybe I shouldn't try to eat him after all."

Just to be on the safe side, the giant decided to test the little man's strength.

"I see you think you're quite the hero," he said, picking up a boulder from the ground, "but can you do this?"

He squeezed the boulder with both his enormous hands and, with a crack and a crunch, a few clear drops of water sprang out and fell to the ground.

"Is that all? Why, that's child's play," said the tailor. From his sack of provisions he drew a round cheese that he had been saving for dinner. To the giant, it looked very much like a stone, but it was fresh and soft on the inside. The tailor gave it a firm squeeze, and a stream of liquid ran into the dust.

The giant was impressed, but he tried not to show it. "Well now," he said, "can you do this?" He picked up another stone and, with a grunt and a heave that shook the hillside, hurled it far across the forest. The stone came crashing down in a distant field and scattered a herd of sheep.

"That's a good throw," the tailor admitted.

Just then, he heard a rustling noise in the bushes beside him. A small brown thrush had been caught in a hunter's snare and was frantically flapping its wings. The tailor reached down and, with a quick movement, freed the bird and clasped it in his hand.

"Of course," he told the giant, "your stone fell back to Earth. I can throw a stone so hard that it never comes down again. Watch this!"

With that, he threw the thrush high into the sky. The bird, rejoicing in its freedom, flew straight up and out of sight. The giant, who thought it was a stone, was amazed.

"So you can squeeze and you can throw, but can you lift and carry?" the giant asked.

His tiny adversary pointed to a fallen tree nearby. It was a hundred-year oak with a massive trunk, knocked over in the summer gales. "Let's you and I carry that oak together," the tailor suggested.

"You go ahead and carry the trunk, which everyone knows is the lightest part. I'll follow and carry the branches and leaves."

The giant agreed, and he heaved the trunk onto his shoulder. He heard twigs snapping behind him, and the tailor shouted, "Go!"

Slowly, the giant staggered forward. Roots dug into his flesh as he strained and pulled, and rough bark scraped his back. Step by step, he dragged the tree forward. Meanwhile, at the other end of the oak, the tailor, hidden among

the leaves, sat comfortably on a branch. "I can go faster, if you want," he called.

The giant staggered on for a few more steps, and then let his end of the oak tree crash to the ground. He was panting from the effort and was starting to get worried. "This truly is someone to be reckoned with," he thought. "If I can't beat him with strength, I'll need to catch him with a sneaky trick."

So the giant smiled his widest and wiliest smile. "We are fellows indeed," he said, as the tailor strolled out from among the oak leaves. "Now the day is drawing on. Why don't you stay in my house tonight and be my guest?"

The tailor happily accepted the offer, and the two walked down the hill to the entrance of a cave where the giant lived. Inside, there was an enormous bonfire blazing higher than a house. Two carved stools were set before it, each one the size of a banquet table. Heaped against the walls were bags of treasure and trophies taken from defeated knights.

There were shields and golden breastplates. A long shelf held a row of dented helmets. Each one was nobly decorated: some with wings, some with plumes and some with bands of gold or silver.

"I love what you've done with the place," said the tailor politely.

The giant was pleased with the compliment, and the evening passed pleasantly. When the stars were shining in the mouth of the cave, the giant led his guest to a bed against the back wall and wished him good night.

The bed was the size of a village green. The little tailor turned this way and that and bunched up the covers, but only when he rolled to the very edge of the bed was he able at last to fall asleep.

Deep in the night, the giant rose to carry out his evil plan. He seized a massive club and crept back to the tailor's bed. He couldn't quite see his guest in the dark, but he aimed a furious blow at the middle of the mattress. With a terrible crash, the bed flew into splinters and kindling, and dust billowed through the cavern.

"That settles that," said the giant, with some relief.

However, his blow had missed the brave little tailor at the edge of the bed. The tailor

He seized a massive club and crept back to the tailor's bed.

waited quietly among the shredded covers and splintered wood. When the morning sun peered into the cavern, and the giant began to stir, he emerged in his nightcap, yawning and stretching lazily.

"Oh," the tailor exclaimed. "A mosquito must have bitten me in the night, for there's a tiny bump on my forehead. I think I tried to swat it, for I've damaged your bed."

The giant stared in disbelief at his little guest, who could sleep through such a terrible blow. "My friend," he said, "a country that holds such terrible tailors as you just isn't safe for giants. I'm leaving, and will never return. This cavern and all the treasures within it belong to you."

And so, without even stopping to put on

his boots, the giant fled with enormous steps over the forest.

The tailor stuffed his sack with rare jewels and precious stones, and took to the road again, the wealthiest man in the kingdom.

He marched on, through forests and fields, his bag of riches swinging at his side. But the bag was heavy and cold, and he began to think that riches weren't everything.

"What's a life without love and affection?" the tailor asked himself. With that, he decided it was time to marry. Now, the loveliest girl in the land was the princess herself. Since the little tailor was as bold as he was brave, he hurried straight to the palace.

He found the princess hard at work in the counting room. She was balancing accounts and writing decrees, and her royal blue gown was speckled with ink.

"Your highness, I'm the tailor who killed Seven With One Blow, and Defeated A Giant, and I ask for your hand in marriage."

The princess liked the look of this proud little fellow, with his easy air and his green and gold sash. But she had a kingdom to run, and she wasn't about to marry just anyone.

"How many giants did you defeat?" she asked. "Was it only one? I have three giants in my kingdom at the moment, and they are causing no end of trouble. If you can beat all three, I promise to consider your proposal."

The tailor agreed and, along with some of the kingdom's bravest knights, he set out to the forest where the giants lived. As they approached, they saw the tall pines trembling, and the leaves on the oak trees shivering. The ground beneath them rumbled and groaned.

"The giants are angry!" whispered the knights, clanking with fear.

"The giants are sleeping," thought the clever tailor. "Wait here," he told the knights. "I'll handle this alone."

With that, he crept in among the trees. Sure enough, beneath the tallest pine, three terrible giants lay snoring like thunderstorms. The little tailor tiptoed between the sprawling arms and clambered over a towering boot. He made it to the pine, and climbed right up to the top. Then, from his sack of treasure, he selected a ruby as big as his fist. Aiming carefully, he hurled it down, and struck a giant on the nose.

"Ow!" moaned the giant, waking suddenly. He prodded one of his brothers. "Baff, why are you pelting me with rubies?"

"I'm not pelting you, Boff," Baff said sleepily.

Now the tailor selected a large sapphire, and threw it at Baff, hitting him in the eye.

"Ooo!" Baff cried, and he shoved the third sleeping giant. "Biff, don't you dare throw sapphires at me!"

"I didn't," Biff grunted. "Let me sleep."

Then, an emerald the size of a goose egg whistled out of the sky and smacked him in the forehead.

"Boff!" Biff roared, "Keep your emeralds to yourself!"

Biff gave Boff an angry blow. Boff kicked Baff – and in a flash, all three giants were punching, biting and bashing each other.

Even half-awake, they were vicious fighters. The tailor clung to his perch as trees crashed down around him, and dark holes opened up in the earth. The giants fought and fought until, at last, the shaking stopped and everything was still.

When the knights finally dared to enter the ruined forest, they found the brave little tailor seated calmly among three dead giants. He was peeling an apple with the blade of his scissors.

The knights rejoiced to see that the kingdom was finally rid of its giants. They lifted their hero onto their shoulders and carried him home in triumph. All the palace folk turned out to cheer him – and the princess, too, was pleased.

"I'm not saying I'll marry you just yet," she told him with a smile, "but I'm seriously considering it."

About the stories

The Gingerbread Man first appeared in an American magazine in 1875. Other versions include *The Runaway Pancake* (from Russia) and *The Little Dumpling* (Hungary).

The Three Billy Goats Gruff and *The Three Aunts* are both from Norway.

The Little Red Hen comes from Russia.

The Mouse's Wedding is from Japan.

Baba Yaga appears in several Russian and Eastern European folk tales.

The Boy who Cried Wolf is from a collection of Ancient Greek fables by a storyteller named Aesop.

Stone Soup is based on an old European folk tale. In some versions, the soup is made with a nail.

Tam Lin comes from Scotland.

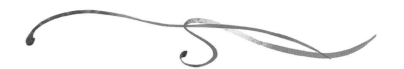

The Bremen Town Musicians, *The Magic Porridge Pot* and *The Brave Little Tailor* were collected by brothers Wilhelm and Jacob Grimm, who lived in Germany around 200 years ago.

The Enormous Turnip is a Russian story by Count Alexei Tolstoy.

The Fisherman and the Genie is from a collection of stories called *One Thousand and One Nights* (also known as *The Arabian Nights*), written around 1,000 years ago in the Middle East.

Chicken Licken was first written down by Danish author Just Mathias Thiele in 1823. It's sometimes known as *Chicken Little*.

The Little Nut Tree is adapted from the popular rhyme 'I had a Little Nut Tree', which might refer to a visit of a Spanish princess to the English king in 1506.

The Ugly Duckling was written in 1843, by Danish author Hans Christian Andersen.

Acknowledgements

Designed by Sam Whibley
Edited by Rob Lloyd Jones and Lesley Sims
Digital manipulation by John Russell and Nick Wakeford

First published in 2016 by Usborne Publishing Ltd., 83–85 Saffron Hill,
London EC1N 8RT, England. www.usborne.com Copyright © 2016 Usborne Publishing Limited.